I0761874

Whom Shall I Fear

Nancy Powell

Book One
The Keepers™ Series

TotalRecall Publications, Inc.
1103 Middlecreek, Friendswood, Texas 77546
281-992-3131 281

ISBN: 978-1-59095-502-4
UPC: 6-4397725021-6

Edited by: Jessica D. Caruso

Library of Congress Control Number: 2015954561

Printed in the United States of America with simultaneous printings in Australia, Canada, and United Kingdom.

FIRST EDITION

1 2 3 4 5 6 7 8 9 10

To my husband and best friend

About the Book

Anna and Bart have been best friends since childhood. Bart is in love with Anna, but she wants to graduate college before surrendering to love. After Anna's parents die, Jaeger, involved with a drug and human trafficking cartel, forces Anna into an illegal marriage and holds her captive. He plans to sell her in South America and take her inheritance after she disappears. Anna escapes, enrolls in college, and finds a job as a live-in nanny for Carol Dugan. Charles and Mary Dugan, Carol's parents, are compassionate Christians who accept Anna as a family member. They support and try to protect her, even after they learn that Jaeger is part of a human trafficking cartel, and he and his friends want to kill Anna.

Raised on an Arkansas horse farm, Anna is an expert with horses, a rifle, and revolver. Although she is often afraid, she uses her skills to protect herself and the Dugan family but relies on God more than her proficiency.

List of Main Characters

Anna Chapman– (POV) Red hair, brown eyes

Bart Grayson – (POV) Brown hair, blue eyes

Mr. Prince – Appaloosa dealer and family friend

Jaeger – Neighbor and Anna's abductor, brown hair, brown eyes, muscular, 6'2."

Cara – Jaeger's mother

Helen – Jaeger's young sister

Charles Dugan — College professor, brown hair, stocky build, a kind Christian man

Mary Dugan – Slim, blond, beautiful, a compassionate Christian woman

Carol Dugan – Blond, blue eyes, Charles and Mary Dugans daughter

Jackie Freeman – Anna's friend, dark hair, brown eyes, slim

Jason – Jackie's boyfriend

Mr. Tucker – The exterminator

Danny – Mr. Tucker's ten-year-old grandson

Jim – Mr. Tucker's fifteen-year-old grandson

Doug Miller – Detective, large man, sandy hair, he becomes a family friend

Polkadot – Anna's appaloosa horse

Curly – Carol's dog

About the Author

Nancy Powell has won several writing awards for short stories and poetry. Dark Secrets (under the name Ollie's Angels) won first place in the 2010 Mainstream Novel category at the Oklahoma Writers Federation, Inc. (OWFI) Contest. Also, the second book in the Ollie's Angels Series won an OWFI award in 2010. Dark Secrets was also awarded the 2012 third quarter Grand Prize at the "Books Without Publishers" writing contest sponsored at www.UltimateHeroContest.com

Nancy Powell is married, the mother of two children, and has seven grandchildren. She is a member of the Church of Christ, River Valley Writers of Fort Smith, Oklahoma Writers' Federation, Inc., Greenwood Writers, and Round Table Poets.

In addition to writing, Nancy loves gardening, sewing, and painting. The paintings and book cover backgrounds in the Ollie's Angel Series are her interpretations in oil paint.

Acknowledgement

I want to thank my family for their love and support, and my writing friends for their help and encouragement.

Chapter 1

Her long red hair waving in the August breeze, Anna leans against a post and gazes across the pasture. She was eleven when a flash flood roared through the valley, threatening to uproot that sycamore. The leafy giant stands beside a lazy creek, still holding her tree house and swing. As each storm thundered in, tugging at roots and thrashing branches, she prayed for her tree. From its shade, she and Dad shot targets along the creek bank, and before her sixteenth birthday, she could hit the center of every bull's-eye. Like that tree, Mom and Dad were supposed to remain. She did not know they were in danger, or she would have been on her knees, praying as never before.

She glances toward the farmhouse. It looks the same as last week, except Mom is not calling from the back door, offering lemonade, and Dad is not here, a hand on her shoulder, giving advice. He was careful. She cannot believe their death was an accident and wonders if Jaeger realized her Dad had suspicions about activities on the nearby farm.

A family friend turns onto the dusty lane. An appaloosa dealer, he promised to find good homes for the horses. Panic tightens her chest at the sight of his trailer. "He's coming for the horses, another chunk of my life." Clenching her teeth, she steps forward.

The slim old man slides from his truck, adjusts a sweat-stained hat, and grabs Anna in a tight hug. "I wish I could help.

I loved your daddy like a brother, and your mama was . . . ."

She pulls away. "Thanks, Mr. Prince, but today, let's not talk about Dad and Mom. I don't want to start crying again." Fingernails digging into her palms, she strides toward the barn. "I fastened the horses in the lot. I'll lead them to your trailer."

"Anna, let me pasture Polkadot while you're away at school. I know how you love that mare."

"I'll be there four years. Just find her a good home." She turns her face away, her lip quivering. "Although, I want to meet Polka's new owners before I sign. She needs someone gentle."

"I'll prepare the papers."

Anna hardens her emotions until the old man drives away. Sitting on the porch swing with daylight fading, she allows tears to flow from her brown eyes. The ranch is quiet—no horses stomping and snorting, or neighing for a colt. There are no lights in the kitchen, no one to ask about her day, or give advice for the future. Even the fat old cat is out hunting.

A pickup turns onto the lane. She stands. "Jaeger! I don't want to see him." Stepping inside, she hooks the screen, takes a bottle of cola from the fridge, and sits at the kitchen table, out of sight from the front door.

The screen door rattles with his loud, demanding knock. "Anna, I saw you on the porch when I turned off the road. I had to work late, or I'd have been here earlier. I know you're upset, but don't shut me out. I came to help."

She clears her throat. "Jaeger, all I need is time. I have a lot of decisions to make."

"You shouldn't make big decisions now. Your mind's confused with grief."

A vision of two flower covered caskets flashes through her

mind, and she gasps, trying to choke back sobs.

"I'll come by after work tomorrow and feed the animals."

She takes a deep breath. "There are no animals. Everything is gone, except my cat."

He slaps the wall. "You—you sold the horses. I wanted some of them."

"Mr. Prince offered a fair price."

She hears him stomp across the porch and kick an empty feed bucket that she should have taken to the barn. It rattles into the yard. "You didn't make an offer—Mr. Prince did."

"But you knew I wanted the stallion and some of the mares. Dad bought forty acres on the north side of this farm. I planned to move them over there."

"That land is covered with brush. You need pasture for horses."

"Has old man Prince paid you?"

Gritting her teeth, she breathes deep. "*Mr.* Prince will pay me when he sells them."

"Tell him you want them back."

"I gave my word." She scoots her chair away from the table, slams the cola bottle against the red-checked tablecloth, and plods across the room, her boots echoing on the oak floor.

"Tell him your fiancé wants you to keep them."

"I am not your fiancée, not even a girlfriend, and I never have been. Dad told you not to come over here again."

"Anna, I know your dad didn't like me, but I can help you through this."

"Goodnight, Jaeger." She locks the wood door, turns on the air conditioner, and sits in the dim kitchen, arranging a pile of sympathy cards that came in the mail. Waiting for Jaeger's truck to disappear, she clicks on a lamp and lifts an envelope from Bart—her best friend.

She remembers the time Jaeger came by and found Bart sitting on the porch swing with her. Jaeger yanked him from the swing, threw him into the yard, and began yelling insults.

She grew up with Bart protecting her. He would have fought to his last breath if Dad had not stepped out with the bullwhip and ordered Jaeger to go. Too bad Bart's leave was over, and the Marines refused to give him more time. She did not want him to join the military and go away, but he said that would enable him to get an education.

Thinking she cannot bear another word of sympathy, she takes the cards to her room and drops them on her desk, beside her last English composition. Seeing the paper, she can almost hear Mr. Wilson's deep voice telling the class, "I'm sick of reading about traffic accidents. Kill your character some other way." She followed his directions, but this story is real. Dropping onto her bed, she cries, "God, change the characters and bring back Mom and Dad."

The next morning, before seven, Anna unlocks her parents' antique shop. The sign on the door states, "Open 9 to 5," but she wants to label things for quick sale. Suzanne, the little girl she watches most evenings, has gone to spend time with her grandmother. Anna can work late.

At five, she turns the deadbolt, closes the drapes, and clicks on the porch light. At six, Jaeger beats on the door. "Anna, if you don't let me in, I'm calling the cops to check on you. I know you're in there. I saw your car through the storeroom window."

Her throat dry, she swallows. "Go away. I have work to do. I don't need distractions."

"I won't get in your way. Come on. Open the door and take this cola before the ice melts. I stopped at the drive-in and got you a large. The least you can do is take it."

* * * * *

Thinking clearer than she has in days, Anna sits on the side of her bed and wipes a strand of hair from her forehead. She wonders if the sheriff has learned anything more about the driver that killed her parents. Green paint was the only evidence found at the scene.

Closing her eyes, she remembers Dad's loving arms and understanding ways. She stands and takes an old stuffed bear from a shelf. He gave it to her years ago. Hugging it, she whispers, "Dad was tough but gentle—taught me to hunt, fish, and was proud when I beat him at anything. Jaeger is tough but mean and jealous of everything. My biggest mistake was letting Jaeger into my life. He took over as easily as if I was—" She opens her eyes wider.

"Drugged! That's it. From the first hour that I let him into the shop and took that Coke, everything is a blur. When he wasn't around, Cara, his hateful mama, was fixing me drinks and giving orders. I had to be out of my head to let them get away with that."

Shaking the bear gently, she continues as if it can hear. "Yesterday I spilled the punch she gave me into the bathroom sink. That's why I was sane enough to disagree with Jaeger last night."

She runs a hand over a worn Bible. "Dear God, I'm a prisoner and only married a few days. I barely remember a wedding. It can't be legal. God, please, please help me get out of this mess. Eve took an apple—I took a cola. I should have known better; Dad and Bart warned me."

Anna looks in the mirror. Her hand trembles as she touches a large bruise puffing the left side of her face. "What did he say about beatings I'll get in South America? South America?"

The exhaust on her father-in-law's old pickup pops as he slows to turn. Gravel crunches when he pulls into the driveway. The chain on the porch swing rattles, and Jaeger's boots stomp out to the truck. She peeks around the curtain as they drive away.

"He's going with his dad and leaving the car." She plops the bear on a shelf, grabs clothes from the chest of drawers, runs to the bathroom, and is dressed quicker than she has ever dressed in her life. She needs to leave before his mama arrives.

The car is hers—a high school graduation gift from her parents—and registered in her name. Jaeger acts as if he owns it, never lets her drive, and does not allow her to have more than five dollars in her purse, joking that she could not get far on five bucks. He does not know that she hid an extra key and most of her graduation money behind a broken piece of sheetrock inside her closet. She shivers at the memory of what he tells her each morning, "Remember, my name means *hunter*. If you run, I'll hunt you down, and you'll die slow and painful."

Many times she has heard her mom quote the 27th Psalm. It comes to her as clear as if her mother were beside her. "The Lord is my light and my salvation; whom shall I fear?"

She pulls out the money and key and looks for her suitcase and overnight bag. "Did he get rid of them?" The fight last night was over her parents' things—he was moving them out of the master bedroom.

After Jaeger hit her, she went to bed with an ice pack on her face and did not watch TV or drink cola. "I wasn't drugged yesterday. That's why I can analyze this." She nods to the stuffed bear. "I have to get out while I can. If I stay, he'll kill me for sure."

"I would have walked away from that wedding, but I couldn't think straight. Jaeger's bratty sister stuck her foot on the tail of my dress and wouldn't move. While everyone sat bewildered, Jaeger's mother laughed. His cousin lifted Helen's foot."

She blinks at the bear on the shelf. "Strange, I don't remember the ceremony, only that incident—her foot on Mama's wedding dress. Who planned it? Who was there? I don't remember. Within days of the funeral, how could I? I wouldn't have—he drugged me. God, forgive me, for I can't help the hate."

Anna crams clothes inside plastic bags, runs outside, tosses them into her red Mustang, and slams the trunk before hearing Jaeger's mama turn onto the lane in her old blue Chevy. Helen, Cara's sullen, look-alike daughter, sits beside her. Anna stands silent, hope sinking.

Cara rolls out, holding a hand against her chest, wheezing. "Last night, Jaeger gave me the key and said I could use his car to go to town. Take those things out of my trunk and put them in his. I'm short of air from rushing."

Suppressing an urge to attack the old woman, Anna holds out her hand. "Toss me the keys." Cara tosses one, then the other, while clinging to her door.

Taking a bag from Cara's trunk, Anna drops it beside the car, with the Chevy key on top. "Oh, something's burning. I bet Jaeger left a pan on the stove." She pushes the button to lock her

Mustang and darts toward the house with Helen following. Slamming the door, Anna twists the lock and runs to turn off a burner under Granny's coffee pot—he broke Mama's glass one.

The house rattles as Helen kicks and bangs at the entry.

Purse on her arm, Anna props a foot against the door, unlocks and opens it enough to turn the lock so it will catch when she steps out. Helen tries to get in, but Anna pushes against her and pulls the door closed. The bolt clicks.

"I want a drink," Helen whines.

"Here." Anna thrusts a bottle of water toward her. "Drink this. I haven't opened it."

"I don't want water. I want cola."

"I don't have any."

"Yes, you do. I saw them yesterday."

"Jaeger drank them."

Helen cries and runs to her mama. "You said I could get a cola from Jaeger's kitchen."

Cara, dragging her feet, plods toward the house, mumbling, "We'll get a drink."

While Helen clings to Cara and cries, Anna climbs into the driver's seat of her Mustang and starts the motor.

Cara turns and yells, "Put those bags in the trunk." She stomps toward Anna. "Get out of that car. Jaeger told me I could use it today."

Anna punches the gas pedal. The mirror brushes against Cara's sleeve. Loud curses echo as the car roars out of the yard, down the lane and toward the highway.

A letter from her parents' lawyer is in her purse. He has a cashier's check waiting from the proceeds of her college fund and Mom and Dad's bank accounts. There will be more when the farm and antique shop sell. She was lucky to get the letter before Cara or Jaeger got their hands on it, and lucky it came yesterday—a day she had sense enough to collect the mail.

She parks in the alley behind the lawyer's office. Maybe Cara will not see the car if she is following. Looking left and right, Anna enters through the back door, gives her name to the receptionist and sits to wait her turn.

The lawyer listens as Anna describes what she remembers of the wedding, and tells a watered-down version of the abusive treatment she received from Jaeger and his family. "Is it possible for me to get an annulment? If not, I want a divorce. Jaeger tricked me. I never loved him. I didn't even like him."

Seeing Anna's bruised face and hearing her explanation, the lawyer calls a friend at the courthouse and gets a copy of the marriage license, and the application faxed to him. He and Anna go over the forms together. Jaeger filled out the license application but did not state her correct age. She was four weeks short of eighteen.

Mr. Aaron promises that he will have no problem getting the marriage annulled. "Anna, if you want, we'll have him charged with abduction and abuse. That bruise proves the abuse." He snaps a picture.

"Thank you; I just want to get away. He threatened to kill me if I left. I believe he's capable, but he shouldn't have a reason when the annulment is official, and he has no claim to my property." Anna leaves with a handshake and a promise to call with her new address.

She stops at a drive-through for a sandwich, swallows two headache pills with a gulp of cola, takes a bite of hamburger and pulls back onto the highway. It is afternoon before she parks in a shady spot at the University of Arkansas. After a deep breath, she whispers, "Stay with me, Mama. Both of us want this."

The asphalt parking lot is like a hot grill. Through thin sandals, her feet burn and she runs to a shade where she can stop in the grass before going into the building. Inside, she stands close to a vent, fans her blouse, and remembers words her mother spoke: "Anna, your dad and I wanted to attend college, but we could never afford it."

Anna fills out a form she gets from a receptionist and stands in line for a counselor.

The man frowns. "You may not get the classes you want at this late date."

She breathes deep and swallows. A tear rolls from under her long lashes. A trembling hand slaps it away. "I filled out papers for classes I want to take. You should have them. I'm sure Mama mailed them."

"Young people amaze me—so smart, but irresponsible."

She dabs at a tear. "I completed the forms. Please, look again. I know she sent them."

"Check with your mama and come back. There's a line of students waiting. You should have sent them online." He frowns and glances at a paper on his desk.

"But a hit-and-run driver killed my parents the week after graduation." A sob escapes her throat.

The counselor looks up. "I'm sorry to hear that." The middle-aged man frowns and hands her a tissue. "Maybe a clerk made an error. I'll cross reference—Chapman, Anna Marie." He punches computer keys. "That's what happened. Someone changed your name to Chopman."

Afraid to trust her voice, Anna reaches for another tissue.

He stares as if first seeing her. "What happened to your face?"

"My husband hit me."

He glances at the computer. "Your application doesn't show you as married."

"My lawyer's getting it annulled." She breathes deep. "After my parents died, I couldn't think straight, and I wound up married. It was a *big* mistake." She shakes her head. "He and his mama planned to cheat me out of my inheritance. He took over my car, wouldn't let me have any money, and tried to keep me prisoner."

"This is not the Stone Age. Husbands can't do that."

"But he did. Today I escaped with my car and went to see Daddy's lawyer. Mr. Aaron said his law firm will get the marriage annulled, sell Daddy and Mama's property and put the money in a trust for me."

The counselor stares at her. "He hit you hard enough to put that bruise on your face?"

She nods. "I disagreed with him. His answer was a fist."

"Do you want to charge him with assault?"

Anna shakes her head. "I want to stay away from him."

He rubs the frame surrounding a photo of a young woman. "I don't usually interfere with family problems, but I had a sister your age. You need to file a police report—get pictures on record, in case he tries to harm you again. My sis thought she could walk away."

She touches the bruise, flinches and asks, "How can I do that?"

"The chief is a friend of mine. I'll ask him to send an officer to take your information. Besides, I have some papers they need to pick up."

"Jaeger ran off all *my* friends." She wipes the corner of her eye. "Call your friend. I'll file a report. Jaeger may try to kill me. He said he would."

The counselor bows his head. "Filing a report is a wise decision, but I don't think you're in danger while on our campus. The University has security officers."

* * * * *

At a military base in Europe, Bart reads a letter from his Aunt Alice.

> Dearest Bart:
>
> Son, I have bad news. Anna and Jaeger got married in a quick ceremony at the church. I wasn't invited, but heard about it and went. Anna seemed to be in a daze. If I didn't know her so well, I would say she was drunk or high on something, but maybe she's still in shock after losing her parents. Jaeger was his usual brazen self. He took her arm and led her from the church as soon as the preacher pronounced them married. She walked as if in a trance, did not smile once during the ceremony and did not toss her bouquet; Jaeger threw it to Helen. I know how you feel about her, but you have to go on with your life. Please don't do something foolish. You are the only child that I will ever have, and I love you. Take care of yourself and pray.
>
> Love,
>
> Aunt Alice

Bart crushes the letter into a ball and yells, "God, why did you let this happen? Anna doesn't love him." He covers his face with his hands and sobs.

His roommate speaks to him, but Bart is grief-stricken. Other friends come into the room, yet Bart is alone in a world of emotional pain—friends cannot reach him. They call his sergeant and the chaplain to calm him.

That night, on his bunk in a dark room, he remembers years of growing up with Anna. At first, she was like the sister he never had and then a best friend. Before either of them realized, he was madly in love but afraid to let her know.

In the early morning, he is still praying, "God, Anna's special. I know she wouldn't have married Jaeger if I'd been there. He's cruel. Please God, watch over her."

Chapter Two

Anna sees the tall officer through the glass, talking to the counselor and holding the information on Jaeger. The air conditioner kicks on and a blast of cold hits her. She shivers.

The counselor returns to sit behind his desk. "Anna, where will you stay until the dorm opens? We need an address and phone number in your file."

She nods. "I'll rent a room somewhere. I want to find a live-in nanny job and go to school at night. I don't want to date. Jaeger turned me against boys."

The counselor gives her a kind look. "Most men are not like you describe Jaeger."

Anna sighs. "I know. My dad was the opposite."

Straightening her blouse, she stands. "Does the college have a job counselor?"

He snaps his fingers. "We do, and one of our professors is looking for a live-in sitter. He and his wife work and don't like taking their daughter out during inclement weather to go to daycare. The child was sick a lot last winter. Do you have experience and references?"

Anna smiles. "I took care of a neighbor's little girl during high school."

"Good." He looks at his watch. "Professor Dugan should be out of class. He'll be in his office by now." Circling a building on a campus map, he writes a room number and hands it to her. "Tell him I sent you, and remember to bring me your address and phone number. If you get a job, we'll have to adjust your schedule. Let me know quickly. Classes are filling up fast."

* * * * *

The professor, a stocky man with brown hair and a warm smile, opens the door at Anna's knock. He points to a chair. "I spoke with your counselor. He told me how you got that bruise." He shakes his head. "Tell me about your previous job and references."

She sits and begins. "My neighbor and her husband ran a donut shop. They enjoyed working together at night and arranged a sleeping schedule, so one of them was always with Suzanne, their four-year-old, during the day. Late in the afternoon, they brought her to my house. I kept her there until almost bedtime, and then took her home, put her to bed, and did my homework. I slept in an extra twin bed until morning when her mother came back in time for me to go home and dress for school."

He gets up and walks to the window. "Was your mother nearby and did she prepare the evening meal for you and the little girl?"

"My parents were busy people. They ran a horse farm and a small antique shop. I cooked supper for Suzanne *and* my family. I'm a good cook." She grins. "Mom started teaching me when I was in elementary school."

The professor taps a pencil on his hand. "My wife's been looking for an older woman to take care of our daughter—someone with the experience of running a household. Our Carol is quite active. Two nannies quit the job. If you haven't made arrangements for an apartment, would you consider staying at our house on a trial basis for a week or so?"

Anna looks at him for a long moment before answering. "I should talk to your wife." She shrugs and grins. "She might not like me."

He glances at the clock. "She'll be on her way home soon. While I call her, fill out this application with reference names and numbers."

Within minutes, Anna is following the professor through Fayetteville to his home on the east side of town. He pulls his SUV into the garage of a large rock house, next to a beige Cadillac. Anna parks her Mustang on the shady side of a wide driveway beside a bed of daisies and marigolds.

The professor opens the front door. Anna steps inside. The clean scents of detergent and lemons greet her. Mrs. Dugan, slim, blond and beautiful, clicks into the entry hall on three-inch heels. Evidently, she is a businesswoman, an elegant lady. With heels, she is taller than Anna's five-foot-five. Her chin slightly raised, she smiles.

A little girl comes running, yelling, "Daddy, look what I painted for you."

Professor Dugan bends on one knee, hugging the child and gushing about her artwork.

Mrs. Dugan reaches for the picture. "Be careful, Charles. That paint was damp when she got in the car. It might stain your suit."

Inside the doorway, Anna stands smiling until Mrs. Dugan extends her hand. "I'm Mary Dugan. You must be Anna. Charles and I want to take you and Carol to a restaurant for dinner unless you have other plans. There's a quiet place not far from here. We can eat while we discuss your possible employment."

"That sounds wonderful."

Anna's eyes are on Carol. She kneels in front of the little girl. "Carol is a beautiful name—it's like a Christmas song."

Carol giggles and swings her small hips from side-to-side; blond curls bounce in rhythm. "My name is a song." She yells the first few words of an old rock and roll tune.

Anna smiles.

Carol clamps her arms around Anna's neck, knocking her off balance. They roll onto the tile floor, giggling. Mrs. Dugan grabs Carol's shoulder and yanks her to her feet. "Carol you can't attack our guest. You need to act like a lady."

Still smiling, Anna stands and holds out her hand. "My name is Anna. Carol, I think we can be good friends."

During dinner, Carol snuggles next to Anna and babbles about painting, toys, and the mean old woman who last took care of her. Anna juggles her attention between the adults and Carol. At one point, while Mrs. Dugan is speaking, Carol pulls on Anna's arm, begging her to go look inside the lobster tank.

When Mrs. Dugan stops speaking, Anna, looking at Carol, puts a finger to her lips and whispers. "We'll go when we finish eating. I have some business to talk about with your mommy and daddy. Okay?" She winks at the little girl.

Carol tries her best to return the wink.

After dinner, back at the Dugan home, Carol shows Anna her room and an adjoining room—her playroom before the previous nanny came. "Anna, you can have my playroom for your bedroom, but I didn't want that old woman sleeping in there. She made growling noises at night and put her teeth in a bowl when she went to bed."

Mrs. Dugan laughs. "Is that why you didn't like her?"

Carol shakes her head. "She made mean faces and told me to be quiet, even at playtime."

Mrs. Dugan sits on Carol's bed. "Honey, do you want Anna to help you get ready for bed? Then Daddy can read you a story. I brought work to finish at home."

The little girl grabs Anna's hand, her blue eyes shining. "Will you, Anna?"

Anna nods.

"She can skip a bath, but make sure she washes her face and brushes her teeth."

"Yes. We'll do that." She winks at Carol.

Carol takes a pair of pajamas from a drawer and runs to the bathroom. "I can dress myself. I don't need help." She slams the door.

Anna stands alone, looking around the bedroom, with its ruffled curtains and bedspread, teddy bears, beautiful dolls, and books.

In pink pajamas, Carol opens the bathroom door with a toothbrush in her hand. "I'll hurry so mama won't get mad. I want her to keep you."

While Professor Dugan reads to Carol, Mrs. Dugan shows Anna around the house.

"I work part-time in a nearby office. If you take this job, we'll expect you here weekdays from eleven to five. That should give you time to take early morning classes, night classes, and the university offers a few on Saturday." Unsmiling, she stares at Anna. "You would not be expected to clean, only keep things neat. A cleaning service comes on Saturday morning."

"I like things neat." Anna looks around. "Your house smells clean, like Mama's."

"Charles said you have a scholarship. Are you sure, you want to work? College requires a lot of time for homework. And do you think your parents would approve of you working?"

Anna looks at the floor and then at Mrs. Dugans eyes. "My parents wanted me to graduate from college. I want the same. I think most students who fail, do so because they party instead of studying." Anna stops to swallow a lump in her throat. "My parents would want me to be happy, and I think I will be much happier here than in a noisy dorm or in a lonely apartment. I'm already crazy about Carol. She's similar to the little girl I cared for during high school. Suzanne was like a little sister to me. I miss seeing her every day."

"What about your husband? Is he apt to come looking for you and cause trouble?"

Anna clears her throat. "He doesn't know where I am. Besides, he was only interested in my inheritance. Daddy's lawyer said Jaeger doesn't have a chance of getting a dime. When he learns of the annulment, he'll have no reason to come around. I don't love him and cannot understand how I wound up married. I wasn't thinking clearly after my parents died."

Mrs. Dugan glances at her watch. "It's getting late. We need to make a decision."

Anna looks at her watch. "I didn't realize the time. I'll leave and let you talk it over, but please consider me. I want the job, and I promise you won't find anyone to care for Carol better than I will." She starts down the stairs, then stops. "I don't have a phone yet, but tomorrow I'll stop by Professor Dugans office to inquire about your decision."

"Where will you stay tonight, Anna?"

She pauses in the entry. "Can you recommend a nice hotel,

moderately priced?"

"I'll ask Charles. He may know."

Waiting, Anna shifts her weight from one foot to the other and considers the home—only one TV in the house but hundreds of books. Every room has a Bible, not gold leafed decorative Bibles but study books, well-worn from searching fingers. Mama warned her about touchy-feely men. Professor Dugan is not that type. His eyes and actions show love for his wife and daughter. He is a man of authority, but Mrs. Dugan runs the house; she and Carol are the ones Anna will need to please.

"Anna, I called the reference numbers you gave Charles. Everyone highly recommends you—especially the couple where you worked and your minister. I'm pleased to know we are of the same faith. Our ministers have known each other for years."

"I'm glad you're Christians. I prayed that you would be."

Mrs. Dugan nods with a smile. "I must work long hours before the new semester starts, and I certainly prefer a Christian to watch Carol. I hate to leave her in daycare for so long. Would you like to stay for a week on a trial basis?"

"I'd love to. Do you want me to bring my things in tonight?"

"Certainly. Give Charles your keys, and he'll bring in your suitcases."

Anna feels her face burning. "I'm afraid it's only a few plastic bags. Jaeger, the guy I married, got rid of my luggage. I packed my clothes in plastic sacks."

"That's fine. You can hang them in the closet of the room next to Carol's."

Within an hour, Anna is ready for bed. She leaves her bedroom door ajar, so she can hear Carol if she should cry in the night. Sliding onto smooth, cool sheets, she sighs.

With a jerk, Anna sits upright. Jaeger's a spiteful person, he can't touch her inheritance, and he doesn't love her, but what if he discovers where she is staying? Forcing Jaeger from her mind, she thinks of Bart, sweet and gentle. She falls asleep wondering what she did with his address.

The next morning, Anna wakes to a giggle. Carol's nose is almost touching her own. "Mama said not to bother you, 'cause it's not time for you to start work, but are you awake?"

Lifting her watch from the bedside table, Anna whispers. "Five-thirty! Carol, you are an early bird, but the early bird gets the biggest breakfast and sings the sweetest song." She pulls on her robe and stands. "Should we wear shorts or jeans?"

"Shorts, pink ones."

"All right, go put yours on, and then we'll decide what to have for breakfast."

"Pancakes. I love pancakes."

Anna grins. She is not sure if she should start cooking or wait for Mrs. Dugan.

"Carol, you'll have to whisper if we go downstairs. I don't want to wake your parents."

They tiptoe to the kitchen. Carol takes pancake mix from the cabinet and slams the door.

"Shh, Carol. It's too early to wake everyone."

* * * * *

Yesterday, Bart woke with an uneasy feeling and worries for Anna. He spent the majority of his day saying silent prayers. Everything reminded him of her. While sawing boards for building, he remembered working on her tree house. At the shooting range, he thought of the crude board targets along the creek. Anna was expert at hitting the bull's-eye.

He finishes his morning prayer with a calmer spirit, grabs the pillow from his bed, hugs it to his chest and whispers, "Oh, Anna, I wish this could be you. I love you more than life, but never got the nerve to tell you."

Chapter Three

Anna turns the last of a large stack of pancakes as Mrs. Dugan comes downstairs, dressed in another suit. Mrs. Dugan laughs and ruffles Carol's hair. "Anna, I don't mind if you want to cook, but don't think it's part of your job. This chowhound would eat pancakes every day if I allowed it. We usually have cereal or eggs and toast. I watch Carol's diet closely. Diabetes runs in her dad's family."

Anna nods. "I'll remember. Do you have specific snacks for between meals?"

"She can eat all the fruit she wants, no more than one slice of cheese each day and eight ounces of yogurt, all the white milk she wants but no chocolate. She can have a few crackers, oatmeal cookies made with fruit and honey, and normal desserts at mealtime. You're welcome to eat anything we have, but please don't bring candy into the house to tempt Carol."

Anna glances at Carol. She has helped herself to a stack of pancakes, smothered them with syrup and has her mouth stuffed full. "I understand. I'll be careful not to give her anything that might endanger her health."

Mrs. Dugan pauses before leaving the room. "You may call me Mary, but you should continue to call Charles, Professor Dugan. If you were not attending the college, you wouldn't need such formality, but the university expects students to use appropriate titles."

"Thank you. I prefer to call him Professor."

"One thing more—we always try to speak proper English

around Carol, no baby talk or slang. We believe teaching at home is important and proper speech when learned in daily interaction will make school easier."

"I agree."

Mary helps herself to bacon, eggs, pancakes, and coffee. "You're a good cook."

"Thank you. Breakfast was Carol's request." She glances at the little girl, still stuffing her mouth. "I'm glad you don't mind me using your kitchen. When school starts, I'll have to rush off to both early morning and evening classes. I've applied for seventeen college hours, but in the meantime, I'll be glad to prepare dinner if you'll tell me what you want me to cook."

"Feel at home. Cook and eat whatever you want. As I said earlier, I'll be working extra hours until school starts. I don't know when I'll be home, but it will be nice to know Charles and Carol have dinner at a decent hour. Meat is in the freezer." She glances at her watch. "I must be on my way. Charles should be along soon."

Tugging at his necktie, Professor Dugan appears in the doorway. "Mary, will you pour my coffee? I have an early meeting."

She pours the black liquid into a mug, before straightening his tie. "Anna made a delicious breakfast. Take a couple of minutes to eat. Your staff can wait."

He sips coffee and reaches for a fork as she sets a plate in front of him. He wolfs the food like a young boy, tugs once more at the tie, gives Mary a quick kiss and hugs Carol. "Be good, sweetheart. Daddy will be home when the fat hand on the clock points to five."

Mary laughs, holds Carol's hands and kisses her forehead.

"Save my hug until tonight when you are not sticky with syrup."

She wipes her hands on a dishtowel and takes a key from her purse. "Anna, here's a key for you. Keep the front door locked unless you are in the front yard. The back gate remains locked, so you don't have to worry about the kitchen door. I allow Carol to play in the backyard whenever she wants. See you this evening."

The door into the garage clicks shut. Anna sits at the bar beside Carol, nibbles a piece of bacon and sips orange juice.

Tilting her head to one side, Carol asks, "Don't you eat pancakes?"

Anna smiles. "I like them with lots of syrup, but too much will make me fat and I'd have to buy new clothes."

"Mama says too much sugar might make me have to take shots."

"Why don't we both try to not eat many sweets. We want to be strong and healthy?"

Nodding, Carol pushes her plate away. "No more sugar."

After they put dishes in the dishwasher, the girls stare into the backyard from the sliding glass door. Looking at large pecan trees scattered across the property, Anna sighs. Squirrels jump from limb to limb and blue-black martins sail across the green expanse. "Your yard is beautiful, but I'm surprised you don't have flowers."

Carol frowns. "Flowers are in front. Daddy didn't want them in the back. He said snakes hide under bushes. I don't like snakes, and I don't like my playhouse anymore."

Anna frowns. "Why?"

Propping her hands on her hips, she wrinkles her forehead and squints. "Cause a big snake with a black mouth was sleeping in my doll's bed. I haven't played in the yard since."

"Did your daddy kill the snake?"

"No. I saw it with my binoculars. It went away before Daddy got home." She shrugs and frowns. "I told that woman, but she said, 'Go upstairs and play.'"

"It must have thought your doll's bed was a good place to sleep."

"Yeah. Mama said it was a chicken snake. They're not poison." She shrugs again. "I can play in the backyard, but I don't want to until it's cold enough for snakes to freeze."

Anna glances at the little girl, clutching her doll. "What is that rock building?"

"Daddy said it's a stable. The man who lived here a long time ago kept his horse in there. I want a horse, but Daddy said our yard doesn't have enough grass."

Anna shades her eyes and scans the yard. A seven-foot rock fence surrounds the spacious home—a massive gate made from a steel plate protects the only outside entrance. "I see why your mother said you could play in the backyard. Only a helicopter or Spiderman could get over such a fence. Does anyone ever open the gate?"

"The man who mows the grass. He has a big tractor with doors and windows. He drives in, mows and drives out. Daddy told him not to leave the gate open while he mows, because dogs might come in."

"Carol, look at that snake. It's chasing a squirrel across the yard." Anna leans forward and points.

"There's another one." Carol squeals, "Oh, poor squirrel."

"Those are not ordinary snakes. Did you say you have binoculars?"

"Upstairs, in my room. I'll get them." She rushes away and returns with a powerful pair of field glasses.

Anna reaches for them and focuses on one of the long gray snakes. "Oh, my! Carol, do you know of anyone around here who keeps snakes for pets?"

"No. I wouldn't want a friend with a pet snake."

"I used to have a book on reptiles, and I've studied them on the computer. That kind does not naturally live in Arkansas. I'm glad you don't want to go in the backyard because they're poisonous. I'm going to call your daddy."

Getting his number from the bulletin board, Anna dials and gets a recording. She tries calling Mrs. Dugan and gets a similar message. "I'll call the University's Science Department; maybe they can tell us what to do."

After several rings, a man's gruff voice answers. "I'm very busy, please call again after two."

"Sir, this is an emergency," Anna shouts.

"Explain."

"Sir, we have two black mamba snakes in our backyard. Do you know anyone who can catch or kill them?"

"Young lady, I don't have time for jokes. Black mambas don't live in the United States."

"Sir, I've studied snakes. I know what they are."

"You've probably found chicken snakes or cottonmouth. Call the police and ask their advice."

Anna hears a click. She calls the police station and tries to explain about the snakes. The receptionist is more abrupt than the person at the Science Department. "Our animal control officer is off today. If the snakes are there tomorrow, call again or call an exterminator."

"What are we going to do? Black mambas will kill anyone entering the backyard."

Carol's eyes open wide. "I heard Daddy tell Mama that he's going to come in the back gate after work and start cleaning out the old stable so you'll have a place to park your car. Do you think they'll bite him?"

Anna nods. "Does he have hunting guns?"

The little girl shakes her head. "You can't touch the guns. We'd get in trouble. Besides, Daddy keeps them locked in a big metal closet."

"Did you ever see him put away the key?"

She nods. "He hid it. I'm not supposed to know."

"But do you know?"

"Daddy will get mad at both of us."

Anna sighs and slaps her hands on the countertop. "Carol, I know how to shoot. My daddy taught me, and I'm a good shot. If I don't kill the snakes, they may bite your daddy when he gets out of his car."

"But if you open the door, will they run in here?"

"I'll shoot from the upstairs window."

"Come on. I'll show you." Carol opens the door to the garage and points to a stepladder. "Daddy climbs on that. It's under the blinking light. The light takes your picture if you get in front of it."

Anna finds a key, goes to the metal cabinet and unlocks the door. "My dad's rifle is like this. I could hit the bull's eye with it every time." She takes a handful of shells from a box, drops some in her pocket, and loads the gun. "Come on, Carol. We need to hurry while they're still in the yard."

After maneuvering the screen from the bedroom window,

Anna looks through the scope, aims, and fires. One of the reptiles writhes on the lawn. The other, with head held high above the ground, races toward the house weaving in a side-to-side motion. She fires. It keeps coming. Again, she fires and hits it below the swaying head. Turning, she sees the little girl with hands clasped over her ears.

Placing the gun on the floor, Anna takes hold of Carol's hands. "They're dead."

"Both? Are you sure?"

"I'm positive." Anna smiles. "Now we need to take this gun back to the cabinet."

Carol runs down the stairs and stands holding the garage door open for Anna. They return to the kitchen and take a bottle of juice from the fridge. The doorbell rings and someone bangs on the front door. "Police! Open up! Police."

"Stay in your chair, Carol." Anna goes to the door and peeps through the magnifier in the center of the door's top half. "Show me your badge."

A man in uniform holds up a shiny symbol.

"What do you want with us?"

"A neighbor called and said she heard gunshots coming from this house. You need to open the door and talk to us."

Anna twists the deadbolt and opens the door. She is relieved to see a woman officer standing beside the man. "I guess it's all right if you come in. My name is Anna. I'm the sitter. That's Carol at the table." She takes a deep breath and turns toward the man. "I'm sure the neighbor did hear gunshots. I shot two black mamba snakes in the backyard."

"I'm John McRae." He nods toward the woman. "My partner is Emma King."

"Hello." Anna nods.

"Young lady, it's illegal to discharge a firearm within city limits."

Anna lifts her chin and looks at his eyes. "I know. I also know that black mambas are deadly. I tried to contact Carol's parents—they were unavailable. I called the University Science Department—they told me to call the Police. The girl there said, 'Our animal control officer is not here today; call an exterminator, or call back tomorrow.' I wanted to kill the snakes before they killed a human."

"They were probably chicken snakes."

"I've studied snakes. Those were African black mambas. They were long and gray with black inside their mouths, and they moved with heads held high in the air. Mambas are deadly—if anti-venom is not quickly administered, a person usually dies within twenty minutes following an attack."

The officers look at each other and grin. The woman takes a notepad from her pocket and asks, "Did Professor Dugan give you permission to use his gun?"

"No. He did not. Since I couldn't get help from anyone with authority, I did what was necessary. Take the snakes and run DNA or whatever you need to do, but be careful. One drop of venom is deadly." With a frown, she turns away, pours a glass of juice for Carol and plops onto a chair.

Carol turns up the glass until the juice covers her lip, drinks, sets it on the counter and runs her tongue over her lips. "Anna, don't you want juice?"

"Grape is too sweet, but I'd give a dollar for a cola."

"Daddy has some in the ice chest he takes fishing—he won't mind if you drink one." She goes to the garage and runs back.

"You don't have to pay the dollar if you'll give me a sip."

Forcing a grin, Anna hands her a glass. "Get me some ice and it's a deal."

While the icemaker grinds, Anna lays her head on her arms, resting on the counter.

The officer leans sideways to stare at her. "Are you okay, young lady? You look pale."

"Too much excitement, I have low blood sugar, but that cola will make me feel better."

He lifts the can, pops the top and pours it into a glass of ice that Carol sits on the counter.

"Miss Carol, do you get your swallow first?"

She nods, sticks a pink straw into the bubbles, takes a long drink, and replaces her straw with a blue one.

Propping her elbow on the counter and chin in her hand, Anna sips the cool drink.

The policewoman reaches for the handle to open the door into the backyard.

"Be cautious." Anna hands Carol a napkin to wipe the grape juice from her mouth. "I don't know how those snakes got here. There could be more."

The woman withdraws her hand. "Do you mind if I take a look through your binoculars?"

Carol lifts the heavy field glasses and holds them out to the woman. "They're mine, but you can use them."

Returning to the door, she peers through the glasses. "John, she's right. I did a report on snakes when I was in tenth grade. She shot both their heads off, but I can see black inside the mouth of the one nearest the house. Chicken snakes don't look like that. Cottonmouths have white inside their mouths. Do you think a terrorist could have released them here? Reports of poison snakes will create an all-out panic if it hits the evening news."

Chill bumps rise on Anna's arms. "Don't give my name to the press, and I don't think the Dugans will want their names on the news."

Tires screech on the driveway. Professor Dugan rushes through the door. Carol runs, reaching to wrap arms around him.

"Are you all right, hon?"

"Daddy, Anna shot two snakes with ugly black mouths. They killed one of our squirrels."

The professor picks Carol up and turns to the officers. "Tell me what's going on."

Anna sips cola while her boss listens to the officer.

"It was fine shooting to hit two moving targets with only three tries." The officer grins. "Under the circumstances, she won't be cited for discharging a weapon within the city."

The professor puts Carol down and drops into a chair, motioning to two other chairs. "Please sit while we talk. I'd like to know how such exotic reptiles got in our backyard."

"We want to know, also. How long have you lived here?"

"We bought last fall and moved in a few days before Christmas. The house sat vacant for years. The rock exterior was in good condition, and so was the wall surrounding the back. We hired a company to remodel the interior. The weather was cold before they added the garage and sunroom. The old stable and backyard are still the same, except for Carol's playhouse. We built it in December."

He shakes his head. "Ironically, my contractor broke through thick rock and concrete to install a drive-through steel gate that seals so tight a worm can't crawl under it, or through a crack. I wanted it tight, so snakes couldn't get in. The house, built before the Civil War, was vacant after the original owner died in the thirties. The owner's only relative lived in Spain. Last year, he contacted a realtor to sell the property."

"Did the previous owner live alone?"

"The realtor thought he had servants, but didn't know what happened to them."

Officer McRae opens the front door but turns before leaving. "I suggest fumigating that stable to destroy eggs or snakes still inside."

"I'll do that, Sergeant."

Anna rubs her hands over the damp glass and wipes her face. "Professor, what will you do about the snakes? Buzzards will fly in if we don't get rid of them."

"You're right. I'll need to . . . ." Frowning, he stares at Anna. "Girl, are you sick? Your face is white."

"This has been a stressful morning." She rubs her hands over the glass. "Are you going to fire me for getting your gun?"

"Certainly not! You saved my life." He wets a hand towel in cold water and hands it to her. "Put this on your forehead, and go rest for an hour. Carol can stay with me."

* * * * *

Bart's sergeant yells, "Grayson, open your eyes before someone gets hurt. These are power tools."

"Yes, sir." Bart steps away from the saw, praying under his breath. "Lord, watch over Anna and help me to concentrate. We have to stay alive. I'll rescue her from Jaeger when I get back to the states."

Chapter Four

Waking, Anna looks at her watch. "Oh no, my first day on the job and I fell asleep." She rushes downstairs.

Carol runs to her. "Daddy's working in the yard. He said I could stay inside. Anna, will you cook fried chicken, mashed potatoes and peach pie for supper?"

"I will if your mama has the ingredients. Let's look for a chicken."

They find a frozen chicken, cut into pieces. Anna puts it in warm water to thaw while she peels potatoes. "Carol, do you prefer green peas or green beans?"

Carol frowns and sticks out her tongue. "I don't eat peas or beans."

Anna winks at her. "I wasn't fond of them when I was your age, but my mama let me have extra dessert when I ate my vegetables. She mashed the peas, mixed them with potatoes and I could hardly taste them. Do you want to try that? We'll both do it—like sisters."

Carol grins and hugs Anna. "All right. We can be sisters."

The meal is almost ready when Anna remembers a book she read where the nanny was not allowed to eat at the table with the family.

Professor Dugan comes in from the yard, his shirt wet, perspiration beaded on his forehead and running down the sides of his face. "The snakes are underground. I'm glad you knew what they were. Otherwise, we might all be dead. Mary has been encouraging Carol to go out there and play."

"Sir, did you clean your gun? I just put it back in the cabinet."

"I cleaned it while you were upstairs, but thanks for asking."

"I'm sorry I fell asleep and left you to do my job. I never take naps, but I haven't slept well since my parent's funeral. I guess it caught up to me. I promise it won't happen again."

He grins. "Saving my life earned you a few hours of rest."

She grabs a potholder and takes the biscuits from the oven. "I have a favor to ask if you don't mind."

"What is it?"

"When I got a chance to leave Jaeger, I ran fast and didn't think about taking anything but a few clothes. The house we were living in and everything inside, except his clothes, belongs to me. It was my Mom and Dad's house. Dad's guns, fishing equipment, coin collection, china, jewelry—everything—I left it all. I want to ask my lawyer what I need to do to protect it. I've only been gone two days, but I bet Jaeger and his mama have already taken most of it."

"Certainly, you can call him. Do you have a list of valuables, maybe pictures and serial numbers?"

"I remember Mom making a list with pictures. She gave one set to the insurance man and put one in the safe deposit box."

"Call your lawyer, now. He should still be in his office. Give him this address and phone number. I'll leave the room."

"I'd like you to listen if you don't mind. If Dad were here, he would listen—I might need advice. Being alone is new and frightening." The muscles in her jaw tighten. "Is this a speaker phone?"

He nods, reaches over and pushes the speaker button while the phone rings.

The lawyer answers on the third ring, "Aaron Law Firm."

"Mr. Aaron, this is Anna Chapman."

"Thank goodness you called. I didn't know where to reach you. Jaeger has been having a fit. I filed the annulment and a petition to prevent him or any of his family from entering the house and outbuildings. You should ask the sheriff or a deputy to go with you to take everything of value and put it in storage. I've seen several situations where the partner that leaves gets their valuables stolen, broken, or burned."

"I don't have a truck to move them."

"Rent a U-Haul."

"I can do that, but I didn't know the sheriff would go with me to move things."

"Usually, they don't, but they will if you tell them you fear for your safety. The officer won't help move anything. He'll simply stand and watch, so get someone to help if you can. I'll call the sheriff and explain your situation."

"I'm afraid to go back into that county. If I go to the Sheriff's Department first, do you think an officer will stay with me the entire time I'm there? Jaeger's mean."

"I remember that bruise on your face. I'll request a bodyguard. When can you get here?"

"Not until Saturday morning. I have a job watching a little girl."

"First thing tomorrow morning, I'll notify the sheriff that you'll be coming."

Anna hangs up the phone, sits in a chair, and begins massaging her temples and forehead. "Why did I complicate my life with scum like Jaeger? I bet his sister has Mom's and my jewelry. He's probably pawned Dad's guns and everything else he could carry off."

"Anything with serial numbers can be traced, and you've only been gone two days."

She jumps up. "I need to get the food on the table. I wish Mary could be home to eat while everything is warm."

Carol runs to the garage door. "She is home." Before Mary gets out of the car, Carol tells her about the snakes, the gun, and the police officers."

Mary does not look happy when she walks into the kitchen.

Professor Dugan puts his arms around her. "Put on a happy face, hon. We're alive—thanks to Anna." He explains the scenario as the girls set the table. "Now, let's celebrate with this wonderful meal."

Mary looks at the table and back to Anna. "Where is your plate?"

"I put it in the sunroom. I figured you and Professor Dugan would prefer family-only meals."

Mary shakes her head. "No, dear. There might be a few times when Charles and I prefer a candlelight dinner alone, but I'll let you know in advance of any special evenings. We want you to be part of our family."

Anna opens her mouth to speak, but all that comes out is a soft cry. Whirling around with her back to Mary, she claps a hand over her mouth, but cannot stop the sobs.

Mary's arms circle her shoulders.

Carol hugs her legs. "Don't cry Anna. We want you to eat with us."

The professor's arms enclose Mary and Anna. "Hey, girls, this hugging is all right, but I'm hungry, and I can smell the peach cobbler. Carol, jump in your chair. I'll get our lemonade.

Anna set your plate there beside Carol."

After the prayer, Carol takes a bite of the mashed peas and potatoes Anna prepared for her. "These are okay, but chicken is better."

The professor finishes his meal and leans back in his chair. "Mary, do you object to Carol and me going to visit my sister? I have two more days of vacation that I need to take before school starts, and you're working on a project you can't leave."

"Margaret would love a visit, but what about Anna?"

"Anna's lawyer told her she needs to take valuables out of her parents' house and put them in storage to protect them from vandals. Anna's home and Margaret's are only about thirty miles apart. Maybe I could help to get Anna's things into a storage building."

"Do you think her ex might cause a problem?"

"There will be less chance of interference on a weekday when he's working. A deputy sheriff will go with us to document everything Anna takes."

Mary nods. "I wish I could go with you, but that's impossible. Although, you should call Margaret so she'll be home." She stirs her potatoes before looking up at her husband. "I hate to say this, but I want you to leave Carol with Margaret before you go to Anna's farm. I don't want Carol caught in the middle of any disagreements."

Carol slides from her chair and takes hold of her mother's arm. "No, Mama. I won't cause any trouble. I want to go with Anna."

Unsmiling, Mary turns to her. "Aunt Margaret's or the day-care center. Make your choice."

The little girl scoots back into her chair, folds her arms and puckers her lips. "I don't want to go to daycare."

The next morning, Anna is up and dressed before dawn. She tiptoes down the stairs and has breakfast ready before the family wakes. She sits at the table sipping sweet coffee and nibbling dry toast until Carol yells, "Anna, where are you?"

Mary rushes from her room to Carol's. Within minutes, the sleepy-eyed family, in bathrobes, sits at the table.

"Charles, I do hope you'll be cautious. I know Anna needs help, but bad dreams interrupted my sleep last night. I've always heard that dreams are in black and white, but in last night's dream a green truck was trying to run you off the road." With a concerned frown, Mary picks up her coffee cup.

The professor grins. "In my dream, it was a giant snake with a black mouth."

Anna takes another bite of toast and a sip of coffee. She searches through past conversations, trying to remember if she mentioned anything about the green paint the police held as evidence in the hit and run accident.

Mary gets up for more coffee. "Anna, I've noticed that you don't eat much breakfast. I'll have to remember to keep plenty of healthy snacks in the house for you girls."

Anna takes her plate to the sink. "Mama always kept peanut butter crackers and fresh fruit. I wake early, but it takes my stomach a while to get ready for food."

The professor and Anna are ready to leave as soon as Mary pulls out of the driveway.

"Carol, did you get your doll?"

"No, Daddy; I'll go get her." She rushes up the stairs.

As soon as she is out of the room, Anna asks, "Professor, do you have a license to carry permit?"

"Yes, but I only use it when we go camping. Are you worried about Jaeger bothering us?"

She looks away and bites her lip. "I'm not sure, but . . . ."

"But what? Is there something I need to know?"

Anna turns and sees a worried look on his face. "Did I tell you about the green paint the police found on my parents wrecked car?"

"No. I don't remember that."

"And I don't remember telling Mary about it. That's why I thought it strange when she dreamed about a green truck trying to run you off the road." She lowers her head and rubs her hands together. "Maybe I should go by myself. I wouldn't want to put you and Carol in danger."

Shaking his head, he pats Anna's shoulder. "Don't worry; we'll be fine. I'll put a gun in the glove box."

"I'll call my lawyer and tell him we're coming today."

They are out of Fayetteville, heading south when Professor Dugan asks, "Where do you think we should rent a truck, and what size should we get."

"I want all Mama's dishes, jewelry, her dining room suite, Daddy's guns and fishing equipment, the rest of my clothes, and a few collectibles. The dining room suite will be expensive to store, but my grandpa made it for Mama out of solid walnut. I hope something hasn't happened to it."

"How big is it? If it's a normal size table with six chairs and a hutch, we shouldn't have to get a big truck."

"Without the extension leaf, it looks normal."

"We could go by and look, but . . . ."

She shakes her head. "I don't want to be there when Jaeger comes home. If we rent one in Russellville and leave the car there, we won't need to spend as much time on the farm. I'm sure Russellville has storage buildings."

He glances at her. "Big trucks take a lot of gas. It'll be cheaper to get one in Conway."

She takes a deep breath. "Jaeger's friend works there. I can pay for the gas."

Long before they get to Russellville, Carol is asleep against Anna's shoulder. They drive for several miles with the professor humming along with the soft music of a Floyd Cramer CD. Occasionally the roar of a truck on the highway nudges Anna back to the present. Nervously, she taps fingers against her leg.

The professor clears his throat. "So I'll know what to expect, tell me what Jaeger looks like."

"He's about six-two, with brown hair and eyes. His shoulders are as broad as a lumberjack's. Girls at school thought he was handsome, but he's mean and selfish. He wears jeans and sleeveless tee shirts in the summer and has a dark tan from working outside."

Professor Dugan grins. "I'm glad I brought my gun."

Anna smiles. "We'll have a deputy on our side."

When they park under a shade tree at the rental lot, Professor Dugan turns to face Anna. "Why don't you let me take care of renting the truck? You can pay me later. Jaeger doesn't know my name and it would be harder to trace us."

Anna nods. "If you don't mind."

"Glad to help. You and Carol stay here until I drive the rental around." He takes the gun from the glove box, tucks it inside his shirt and walks away.

Anna is telling Carol a story when a big truck groans around the building. The professor is driving.

Carol bounces in the seat. "He looks funny in that big thing."

Anna locks the car doors, takes Carol's hand, leads her to the truck's passenger side and helps her up. "Professor, I'm glad you're here. I've never driven anything bigger than a pickup."

"There's not much difference. This truck has an automatic transmission. You simply guide it down the road."

She looks out the window at the side mirror. "This is bigger than I expected. I'm sure we can move what I want in this. I just hope Jaeger hasn't gotten rid of everything."

Looking straight ahead, Professor Dugan asks, "Anna, what do you plan to major in at the University?"

Noticing the abrupt subject change, she glances at the serious look on his face and realizes he does not want Carol to get frightened. "History and natural science, but I've considered archeology. I would love to study the ancient history of this country, but I don't know if it's a profession that would buy groceries and pay the rent. Mom and Dad liked antiques and history—I guess they sparked my interest."

"A Civil War battle was fought on land near our home. Many fine homes built with lumber burned during the war. Our house may have survived because it's rock. I've heard the man who built it was a sea captain, and before the war, he brought slaves to the South from Africa. The Confederate Navy conscripted him and his ship during the war. I don't know why he settled in Fayetteville, but I heard he died a bitter old man."

Anna leans forward to face Carol. "He might have dropped gold coins in the yard, or maybe he buried treasures. Dad and I owned two metal detectors. We took them to the beach one year and found money, a ring, and lots of junk. If they're still in the barn loft, we'll take them with us and hunt for treasure next week—if your dad doesn't mind."

The professor chuckles. "Sounds like fun. What percentage do I get?"

Carol wrinkles her nose. "What does that word mean?"

He laughs. "How much of the treasure do I get?"

Carol gives him a tough look. "You don't get any unless you help dig for it."

"That's fair. You girls can split the profit unless you find gold, and then I get a third."

Leaning back and closing her eyes, Anna remembers hunting for treasure with Dad and Bart. Dad preferred thinking of horses and the farm, but Bart loved searching.

They drop Carol off at her aunt's house in Mayflower and head for the Sheriff's office in Conway. "If we can avoid it, I think it best not to tell anyone where I work—introduce me as Chuck, a friend from Little Rock. It's true; I was born there."

* * * * *

"Bart Grayson, wipe that miserable look off your face and go into town with us. We're going to have some Friday night fun."

"Thanks for asking, but I don't drink or gamble."

"We're not doing that either. We plan to find girls."

"No, thanks. I'm going to the library."

"I can't believe you. Pining for a married woman is worse than anything we'll do."

Bart's voice is gruff. "I said no thanks. I have homework in the class I started."

Bart takes the letter from Aunt Alice out of his duffel. He reads it again, hoping it will not say that Anna married Jaeger, but it did not change. His eyes fill with tears.

Chapter Five

In a patrol car, a deputy waits to escort Anna and Professor Dugan to the farm.

The first thing Anna notices inside the house is the open hutch without Grandma's china. Panic struck, she runs to the master bedroom. Mom's jewelry, the coin collection, and Dad's guns are gone.

Tools, various farm and garden equipment, and three saddles are missing from the barn. Anna climbs into the hayloft and rushes to the north corner. The metal detectors are still there. She rubs a dirt clod from the bottom of the largest machine and turns away to brush at a sudden tear—that was Dad's machine.

Anna calls the insurance agent and asks him to fax a copy of Mom's list of valuables, with pictures and serial numbers, to the sheriff's office. Professor Dugan and Anna eat lunch in a nearby diner while the sheriff gets a search warrant for Jaeger's family farm.

The sheriff and another officer escort Anna to Jaeger's home to look for stolen items. As they pull into the yard, Helen goes to her playhouse wearing the chiffon dress that Anna wore to her senior prom. The tail of it is brown from dragging in the dirt. So are the matching shoes.

China dishes, jewelry, and two of the four guns are inside Jaeger's home. One saddle, and Dad's tools and equipment, marked with tiny initials, are in the barn. "Officer, they have a garden and a small barn in the woods." She points. "Over there.

I noticed it once when I was looking for a horse that got out through a broken fence."

The officer lifts his eyebrows and grins. "A garden in the woods—what are they growing?"

Anna shrugs. "I didn't go close. From a distance, it looked similar to okra."

Where an officer ordered her to stay, Cara sits on the porch swing and glares at Anna.

The officers are still collecting evidence when Jaeger and his dad come home. Neither speaks to Anna, but Jaeger squats in front of the porch swing to whisper with his mama.

Jaeger stands and leans back with thumbs stuck in the pockets of his jeans. With a cocky grin, he tilts his head a little to one side. "Officer, that stuff was taken from my home. My wife abandoned it when she left."

The officer does not look impressed. "Young man, we have date-stamped pictures of her face after you beat her. She filed charges. We also have a copy of her lawyer's notice of annulment proceedings, along with a court order for you to leave the house. Also, you were notified that theft charges would be brought against you for any of her property taken, given away or damaged. Put your hands behind your back." Handcuffs click. "You have the right to remain silent . . . ."

The deputy turns to Jaeger's parents. "Unless you return her possessions in good condition, you will most likely be charged as an accessory to the theft of property. If you know anything about the remaining assets, it will be in your best interest to give us that information now."

Jaeger's dad mumbles, "You'll have to ask Jaeger. We didn't take her things."

After the sheriff and his deputies finish documenting the recovered, missing, and damaged property, Anna and Professor Dugan load salvageable goods into the U-Haul. A deputy takes more pictures and lists the majority of assets left on Anna's farm.

By the time proceedings at the farm are completed, the sun is hanging low. The professor climbs into the truck while Anna locks the house.

Wiping perspiration from his face with a handkerchief, the professor sighs and looks at Anna. "The storage units will be closed before we get to Russellville. If you don't mind sharing a room with Carol, we can spend the night at Margaret's and drive home in the morning. She has two spare bedrooms."

Anna looks at her jeans. "My clothes are filthy, but if I can get a shower, I'll be fine."

"There's a shopping center before we get to her house. I'll give you a few bucks to run in and buy yourself a change of clothes. Then, you can watch the truck while I get myself a few things."

She nods approval. "I have money for my clothes, but are you sure your sister won't mind us dropping in?"

"Margaret will be glad to have us stay. I'll call to make sure." After talking for several minutes, he clicks off his phone. "She's happy that we'll stay and said Carol has lots of things to tell us."

Nodding before they get to the house, Anna talks to keep herself awake. "Jaeger disposed of some things, but I feel better than I did on the way down. He didn't say a word to me; still I could see the hate in his eyes."

"This will be over soon, and you can forget about him."

She nods. "I found a bottle of pain medicine and a bottle of unlabeled capsules in the small bathroom which Jaeger used. The prescription label shows Cara purchased the pain pills. I don't believe Jaeger was taking it. I think he and Cara were doctoring my cola and juice. She came every morning while he was working. Always, within a few minutes after she got there, she used Jaeger's bathroom and washed her hands before helping herself to drinks from our fridge. She insisted on fixing me one and waited until I finished mine so she could clean the glasses. She was never helpful with anything else."

"It sounds like you may have been lucky to escape when you did."

"I was more than lucky to get away. I feel blessed."

* * * * *

"There's Carol, on Margaret's porch." He chuckles. "She's ready to tell us a million things."

Carol runs into her Daddy's arms. "Aunt Margaret took me to the zoo. We saw bears and a big elephant."

"Hold on. Hold on. Can you let me wash up before you tell the rest?"

She nods and turns to Anna. "Did you find the machines for hunting treasure?"

"I found two; a small one for you and a big one for me."

Aunt Margaret, a plump, gray-haired woman, hands her a damp hand towel. "Here's a cloth to freshen your face. You can scrub your hands with antibacterial soap at the kitchen sink. I hear the shower water, but we'll get food on the table while Charles is getting dressed."

Anna whispers to Carol, "Did you request fried chicken and chocolate cake?"

She giggles and nods.

After they put away the dishes, Anna excuses herself, goes to shower, and then to bed.

She wakes to the scent of coffee and baking bread, washes her face in cold water, and slips into the tee shirt and jeans she bought at the shopping mall. She rolls cuffs in the too-long jeans and goes to the kitchen.

"Good morning." Aunt Margaret gives her a sweet smile. "If you drink coffee, help yourself. We're ready to eat."

Aunt Margaret is a true southern cook. Blue-trimmed dishes surround matching bowls of scrambled eggs, white gravy, butter, strawberry jam, and platters of ham, hash-brown potatoes, and fluffy biscuits.

Professor Dugan says grace and they begin the feast.

Aunt Margaret looks at Anna's plate. "Child, are you sick? You hardly ate anything last night, and you're only nibbling this morning."

Anna smiles. "Last night, I was too tired to eat. This morning, I don't want to overload my stomach. I get car-sick, and we have a long way to go."

"There's enough ham there to make all of you some snacks for the road. You may get hungry before you get to Fayetteville."

Carol lets her milk glass bump against the tabletop. "Aunt Margaret, may I have cake for my road snack?"

"Certainly. I'll wrap each of you a slice."

With the snacks packed, everyone waves and Professor Dugan backs the truck from the driveway. Carol falls asleep against Anna's shoulder before they get to Russellville.

"Professor Dugan, are you still going to have an exterminator to spray the stable? I'm afraid there might be snake eggs in there. Baby snakes are as poisonous as the big ones; they merely have less venom. Maybe, under and around Carol's playhouse should be sprayed, as well. In the wild, mambas choose an animal burrow or an abandoned ant hill to lay their eggs. Here they would probably choose a place underneath the playhouse or an old stable."

He frowns and glances sideways at her. "I don't know much about snakes and only what you've told me about mambas. I'll call an exterminator tomorrow. I intended to do that today, but this trip took precedence."

She leans her head back. "It may not be necessary, but I'm afraid to let Carol play out there until we check the stable for the possibility of a nest."

"Keep her inside next week. I'll call an exterminator Monday morning."

"The territory where mambas originally live is warmer than Fayetteville, but I'm sure they could hibernate under that old stable and survive. I hope none escaped into the neighborhood."

"I don't think they did unless they tunneled under the foundation, and it goes deep."

She smiles down at Carol and moves her, so her head rests against Anna's shoulder. "She's eager to look for buried treasure. I hope she's not too disappointed."

"She is excited. I can imagine dreams of gold coins jingling in her head. This morning she asked me if she could get cowgirl boots and jeans, to wear when hunting treasure with you."

Anna grins. "She saw the western clothes I wore to the rodeos and said she wants some like mine. I can take her shopping for jeans and boots if you want. I believe we could get her a complete outfit for less than a hundred dollars—she'll need jeans and boots when the weather turns cold."

"Talk to Mary. She does the shopping for all of us."

"I'll do that."

Mary thinks it is a wonderful idea for Anna to buy jeans and boots for Carol. "I'll give you money on Monday. Maybe, on your way to the mall, you can stop by and see where I work."

Monday afternoon Carol almost knocks Mary down with excited hugs. "Look, Mama. I have boots, jeans, and a hat, just like Anna has in her room. They're for hunting treasure, and cowgirls wear them too. Anna used to ride horses. She rode her horse Polkadot in rodeos."

Mary sits on the couch as Carol shows her the flat heels on her leather boots. "Anna said flat heels are better for walking. See my jeans? They have glitter on the side and my shirt matches. Anna said I look like a cowgirl queen."

"You surely do. Keep them on until your daddy comes home. Maybe he'll take us to the next rodeo, and you can wear your *Cowgirl Queen* outfit."

"Mary, dinner's ready. I need to go to the bookstore and to the library while you're here with Carol. I ate and put my dishes in the dishwasher. Carol ate one piece of meat and a serving of potatoes but said she would eat dessert with you."

She picks up her purse and removes keys. "The library closes at nine. I'll be home shortly after."

Mary lays her hand on Anna's shoulder. "Try your best to park close to the library entrance and under a light. It'll be dark at nine. Are you certain you ate enough? I can save you a plate on the stove."

Anna smiles. "Thank you, but I ate plenty."

With her list of classes, she enters the bookstore to search for textbooks. Looking at one of the new books, she whistles soft and low.

An unfamiliar voice comments, "You and me."

Feeling her face getting hot, Anna whispers. "I didn't mean to whistle out loud. I'm shocked that books cost so much."

A girl with dark hair and brown eyes smiles at her. She picks up a book like the one Anna is holding. "So am I. I'll have to get a job or eat Ramen noodles all year."

"Maybe they have some used books." Anna finds one on a lower shelf. She turns it over and thumbs through it. "It looks new, except for where someone wrote a name. You can have it."

"Are you sure? I hate to take it when you found it."

Anna nods. "I think my scholarship will pay for books. By the way, my name's Anna. What other classes are you taking?"

She holds out a list. "My name's Jackie."

Anna reads aloud, "American history, biology, chemistry, English II, and algebra." She giggles. "Look at my list."

Jackie glances at it. "You have exactly the same ones. Maybe we'll have some together."

"That would be nice, but I requested American history and English as night classes. Those are my favorite subjects. They'll be easier than math or science in the evening when I'm tired. I have the other three during the day."

"I'm taking algebra on Saturday. A friend told me the teacher is the best one here. He teaches at a high school during the week and is patient when students need help. You should go to your counselor and request that Saturday class unless you're a whiz at math."

"I don't know if he'll do it. He's already changed my schedule so I can work in the afternoon."

She shrugs. "You can try. I have chemistry on Tuesday and Thursday at eight in the morning, and biology on Monday, and Wednesday at eight. Lab classes for both follow immediately after. Friday will be my study day.

"Looks like we'll have chemistry and biology together. I'll go see my counselor in the morning about the Saturday class. Do you know anything about the other teachers?"

"No, but I'm hoping they're good. I need to keep my grades up."

"So do I."

"Hey, a few counselors are here tonight. As soon as I pay for these books, I'll walk over with you to see if yours is here. A Saturday class will fill up fast."

"Great. If he reserves the class for me, I'll get my books tonight."

While Jackie waits to pay, Anna looks for used books. Finding three good ones, she takes an empty bag from the counter and writes her name boldly on the outside with a black marker. While the cashier waits for a girl to write a check, Anna asks, "Can you hold these for an hour?"

The girl looks very tired, but she smiles. "We can hold them until closing tonight. If you haven't picked them up, we'll return them to the shelves in the morning."

"Thank you. I'll be back."

The counselor, whom Anna spoke with on her first day at the University, sits at a desk. Another student walks away as Anna approaches.

"Hello, Anna. It's good to see you again. Professor Dugan is pleased with how well you get along with little Carol. How can I help you tonight?"

She explains about the Saturday class and asks if he can adjust her schedule.

He turns his head slowly. "Maybe, if the one you want is still available." He looks at his computer, bites his lip and drums his fingers on the desk. "I'll write it up, but you need to stick with this one."

"I will." She clasps her hands, and almost squeals, "Thank you!"

Jackie lingers near the bookstore until Anna comes out. "Did you find a history book?"

She nods. "It looks new, but I watched the clerk scan it. It showed used. Algebra and chemistry will be the classes I'll need to concentrate on, so I plan to read through my history book before classes start."

Jackie gives her a thumbs up. "I'm eager to get started. Have you been to the library?"

"Not yet. I planned to go tonight, but it's getting late. I'll go tomorrow evening."

"It's nice. Maybe, I'll see you there. The little apartment I rented has windows on the west side. It gets so hot that the air conditioning doesn't cool it much until after dark. The library is comfortable—I go there almost every afternoon to read."

"I'm a history buff. I want to find local information about the Civil War."

"Interesting. Do you mind if I research with you? I need something to do. Fayetteville is a lonely place if you don't know anyone. I've checked almost every business within a mile for a part-time job, but no luck. I worked in a doctor's office before, although I don't know of any medical facilities within walking distance of my apartment." She clenches her teeth and frowns.

"I sold my car to pay college expenses—not having transportation is a big disadvantage."

Looking at her watch, Anna says, "I have to get going. Thanks for your help. I'm glad you like history. I think we'll have fun investigating old records." She waves and starts toward her car, but turns quickly. "Jackie, is it far to your apartment? I can give you a ride."

"Eight blocks, but I don't want to trouble you."

"Hey, I'd hate to carry that load of books for eight blocks. Come on. It's no trouble."

"I should have taken a dorm room, but I was trying to save money. This winter, it'll be cold walking that far."

Anna turns to look at her before starting the car. "I was told that first-year students, not living with family, have to stay in a dorm or get special permission. How did you get around that?"

"My landlady is an aunt, a great-aunt. I just didn't tell the school that I'm paying rent."

"I'm lucky to work for the Dugans. They are good Christian people and treat me like family. I have a private room, and I don't have to worry about buying groceries."

* * * * *

Bart rests on his bunk, staring at the ceiling while talking with a friend. "It's almost time for fall classes at the University of Arkansas. That was Anna's greatest dream, but Jaeger won't let her go. What could have made her decide to marry him? The one time I kissed her, she pulled away saying, 'I have to wait. We can only be friends until after college. We have to graduate.' Now she's married."

He beats a hand into his palm. "I know he tricked her."

Chapter Six

The scent of apples and cinnamon greet Anna as she walks into the Dugans' house.

"Anna," Carol yells. "We made muffins. Mama let me break the eggs. I only let one shell fall in the mix."

Dropping books onto the couch, Anna takes Carol's hand and they walk into the kitchen. "I didn't know I was hungry until I smelled those. Is this a special occasion?"

Mary nods. "A missing Anna event—baking was a good diversion. Did you find all your books?"

Carol climbs on a bar stool, wraps her arms around Anna and squeezes just as Anna answers. "I d-did."

Mary grins. "You should grab a muffin before they disappear. Carol and Charles devoured the rest."

She reaches for one with a nut on top and places it on a clean saucer. "I changed my algebra class to Saturday. I met a girl named Jackie while looking for books—she told me about the class. According to her, Mr. Brown is the best math teacher on campus. I'll have three classes with Jackie, and I'm going to meet her at the library tomorrow night to research the history of this area."

"Is Jackie from Fayetteville, or does she live in a dorm?"

"She didn't say where she's from, but she rented a one bedroom apartment eight blocks from campus. She's looking for a part-time job in the afternoon that's close enough for her to walk to work. She sold her car to help pay expenses." Anna reaches for her muffin but discovers an empty saucer.

Carol giggles and slides the last fragrant cake toward her. "We made these with applesauce and honey." She shakes her head. "They won't make you fat."

Mary brushes crumbs from the counter into her hand. "What kind of work is Jackie looking for?"

"She'd like to work in a doctor's office or a medical clinic—that's what she did before, but none, close enough for her to walk, are hiring."

"My office is going to hire someone to work four hours in the afternoon to make copies and run errands. Do you think she might be interested?"

"Probably. Your office is only four blocks from her apartment. Anna glances at the clock. I should run over and tell her now so she can apply tomorrow. I'll come straight back."

"I'll drive you over and wait in the car. Charles can put Carol to bed."

"That's a lot of trouble for you. I'm not afraid."

Mary loops an arm around her shoulder. "I'm afraid for you. I've never known Carol to get so attached to anyone outside the family. We can't afford to lose you."

Anna takes a deep breath and wraps her arms around Mary. "Thanks. I can't believe I've found such a wonderful family. Angels must have arranged this."

Mary smiles and reaches for her purse. Anna lifts her muffin. "Do you mind if I give this to Jackie? She's so thin. I bet she's cutting corners on groceries to save money."

"Not at all. There's a leftover pork chop in the refrigerator. Take it, too."

Tuesday evening, when Anna gets to the library, Jackie is waiting in the foyer. "Anna, I got the job, and I worked six hours today. Thanks, for coming to tell me last night. I ate the pork chop before going to bed—it was delicious. The muffin was my breakfast; with a glass of milk, it was fantastic."

"I'm glad you liked them."

"I was hungry. My cabinet is bare, except for stale crackers and peanut butter which have to last until Friday afternoon, when my mom's coming to visit."

Anna frowns. "You should have told me last night. I would have brought you something to eat tonight."

"I couldn't. Mom didn't raise a beggar."

"Does she know you're broke and out of food?"

Jackie shakes her head. "If she did, she'd be here with every dime she could scrounge."

Anna looks down. "That's the way my mom was."

Jackie stares. "Was?"

"Yeah." She turns away. "Last May, both my parents were killed by a hit and run driver."

"What awful luck."

"The worst, but I try not to talk, or think about it. If I keep busy, I can hold off most of my tears until late at night, or when I'm in the shower."

"I understand. If you ever want to talk, cry or scream, you can use my shoulder. Otherwise, I won't bring it up." She slaps Anna on the back. "Let's see what we can find in the historical section."

Within an hour, Jackie has found an article about Civil War battles in and around Fayetteville. Anna finds one about a sea captain who sailed his ship for the Confederates.

"Jackie, do you think they'll let us borrow these books?"

"We can try. I've already got my student card." Jackie goes

to the desk while Anna thumbs through more books.

Grinning, Jackie says, "She let me check them out overnight."

"That doesn't give us much time. I'd love for the Dugans to see these."

Jackie shrugs. "Take them with you. I'll recheck them later. I won't have time to read tomorrow. I'm scheduled to work all day."

"Then, do you mind if we go on? It should be cool in your apartment after the rain."

"You go on. I want to see if I can talk to a counselor and get my history and English classes changed to the evening."

"I'll read while I wait, and then I'll drive you to your apartment."

Jackie takes a deep breath and smiles. "I'm so glad I met you."

"Hey, friends help each other."

Jackie comes out of the counselor's office with a big smile and dances up to Anna. "I have the same class schedule as you. Maybe we can study together."

"Great." Watching Jackie dance, Anna giggles.

"I'm ready to go. You need to get home before curfew."

Anna turns with a frown. "Jackie, I know you were teasing, but the curfew is my own doing. In the few days that I've known the Dugans, they've been like adoptive parents. I don't want to do anything to worry them."

Jackie holds out her hands, moving them from side to side. "Erase what I said. I was only teasing, but I was wrong to tease about someone who cares. Most people would have saved a pork chop for their lunch or given it to the dog. I'll never again tease about such a thing."

Anna stops her car in front of Jackie's door. "If you like bananas, take these. I brought them for a snack inside a study room but forgot to take them in."

"Breakfast." Jackie lifts her chin and grins.

Anna looks up and down the Dugans tree-lined street before reaching for the car's door handle. Seeing movement behind a bush, she scoots lower against the leather seat. A neighbor's light colored dog appears. Anna lets out her breath, jumps out and runs to the house.

Once inside, she shows the articles to Mary and Professor Dugan before going upstairs to say goodnight to Carol. Coming down the stairs, she detects the excitement in his voice.

"Look at this Mary. It says neighbors suspected the old sea captain of holding prisoners. They saw men come in and never leave." He shakes his head and shifts the book to his other hand.

"A crazy man, found wandering in the hills, claimed he was held prisoner in a stable behind a rock house. He said the old sailor living there threatened to turn poison snakes loose to kill anyone attempting escape."

"Charles, that was over a hundred years ago. Surely, you do not think those snakes could have survived."

"Not the same ones, but the species might have. Until last winter when we installed that remote controlled gate, there was no way to get out of the backyard except through the house. Snakes couldn't get over or under a fence like that. The yard provided enough birds and squirrels for food, plus crickets, grasshoppers, and occasionally a neighborhood cat."

Mary places her book on the coffee table. "Did you ever call an exterminator?"

"He's supposed to come in the morning. I'll go to work after he leaves."

"Sir," Anna interrupts. "Do you have some sharp garden hoes? On the farm, I killed several chicken snakes with Mama's garden hoe. I wouldn't be afraid to chop at a baby mamba, or mangle a nest of eggs."

"There's a couple in the garage, but I doubt they're sharp."

"Do you have a file? Daddy taught me how to sharpen tools."

He shakes his head. "I don't know. I grew up in the city, but I have a box full of my dad's things."

"Listen, you two hunters, I don't want Carol in the yard until you are positively sure that no snakes are out there."

"She can watch from the upstairs window. She's afraid of snakes and won't go out."

The next morning, after breakfast, Anna sits at one end of the front porch pushing a rusty file over a dull hoe. When the exterminator arrives, Anna has two sharp garden tools ready to chop at any creature escaping the stable.

In green coveralls, a small elderly man greets Anna. "Is this the residence requesting an exterminator to kill spiders, scorpions, and snakes?"

"This is the place. Are you sure your poison is strong enough to kill snakes?"

"I've got the stuff to kill anything that walks, crawls, or flies. Just point me to the area where pests are living."

Professor Dugan comes to the front door. "Let's get in your truck and drive around to the gate. My wife doesn't want anyone toting chemicals through the house."

Carol runs upstairs, opens the blinds and props her arms on the windowsill.

Anna follows her. "Don't come downstairs until I call you. Your mama said if you stay here until all is safe, we can make oatmeal cookies with raisins and nuts."

Carol's blue eyes are wide pools of worry. "I'll be here 'till you call."

Anna takes the two hoes from the garage and walks through the kitchen. Smiling, she remembers her grandmother's warning, "Never take garden tools in the house. It's bad luck."

Approaching the stable, she hands one hoe to Professor Dugan.

The exterminator pulls a mask from his truck; it looks like something from an outer-space movie. Next, he takes out a large flashlight. "This light is extra bright. Don't look at it, or it will temporarily blind you. It'll do the same to any critters inside. While they're blind, I'll spray them with a deadly gas. You can't come inside without a mask like mine for at least eight hours. For snakes and scorpions, I recommend you leave it closed for twenty-four hours."

He opens the stable door and shines the light inside. "Professor," he yells. "You didn't tell me you still have hay stored in here. Since you think you might have rattlers, I'll need to spray it twice—once after the hay is cleaned out."

"Fine. I want to make sure everything in there is dead. I've been afraid to go in after the stories I've heard. Rumors are that there's a full basement underneath. Poke around a little. If you find a hole or trap door, shoot it full of gas."

"That'll be expensive. This gas is pricey."

"Fill it full—I don't want anything to escape."

"Usually, I find lots of mouse and rat droppings inside old buildings such as this, but since I don't see any in here, I'll almost guarantee you're right about the snakes." His voice gets loud. "Something moved. Shut the door and get back."

Professor Dugan closes the door with his hoe. "Run, Anna. Get in the house."

Like a giant reptile, the hose discharging the poison hisses and thumps against the ground. Anna runs but, when the portable generator backfires with a loud pop, she stumbles and almost falls. After regaining stability in her stride, she looks back—the professor is still stumbling. She reaches out her hand.

"Goodness gracious, I thought I was shot when that thing popped."

Inside the kitchen door, Anna leans against the wall laughing and gasping for breath. "Me too, sir. Me too."

For what seems like an hour, the hose bumps, thumps, and hisses. The generator pops two more times before the man comes outside, shuts off the machine, tosses the mask into his truck and slips out of the coveralls. Wearing jean shorts and a white tee shirt, he sits on the tailgate of his truck. Anna and Professor Dugan walk over to him.

After a few deep breaths, he speaks directly to the professor. "There was something in there, probably snakes, but they should be dead. Do you want me to clean out the hay? It's the same hourly rate whether I'm spraying or raking. Of course, you have to pay for the gas when I'm spraying."

"Clean it out. I have to work the rest of the week. I'd like to burn it all, but this area has a burn ban. I'll have a dumpster delivered to hold it. Anna will have the remote control to open the gate. Call when you're ready to drive in."

He takes another deep breath. "There is a basement. I didn't go down, but I could hear movement. I sprayed a lot of gas in there. I doubt anything could live through it. Still, if you want, I'll spray it again after the hay's removed."

"Do you think it's necessary?"

He nods. "If there are any holes in the wall where snakes can tunnel, they might not get enough gas to kill them. My suggestion, since you've gone to the initial expense, is to go all the way. Once rattlesnakes get burrowed in, they're hard to eliminate."

"Do what you have to; get rid of them. I have a little girl to think about."

Again, he nods. "If you can, get the dumpster delivered on Monday morning and give me a call. I'll be here in the afternoon to clean out the hay and spray again. On Thursday, I'll bring a couple of boys and clear the basement. I hope there's not hay down there."

"It would have been cheaper to toss a bomb inside."

The exterminator laughs. "I knew a guy who did that. It cost him ten times what this will cost, plus he spent time in jail."

Before Professor Dugan returns to work, he suggests meat loaf with mashed potatoes and green peas for dinner. Anna cooks it, but she and Carol eat potatoes, peas and salad. For dessert, they have oatmeal raisin cookies. Mary insists that Anna take Jackie the leftovers.

Jackie squeals when Anna hands her the plate of food. "I love meatloaf, especially with ketchup baked on top."

"I'm glad. Meatloaf and liver are two things I don't eat."

"Yum. This is good."

Anna sits in a wobbly chair at Jackie's table.

Her mouth full, Jackie mumbles, "Careful. These chairs came with the furnished apartment. They're about to fall apart."

Anna stands and turns the chair left and right. "They need

re-glued. Once, I helped Daddy fix our chairs. Get a bottle of wood glue, and we can make them good as new."

"Really! You know how to repair chairs?"

It is after nine when Anna rushes home. Mary is in the living room reading a book.

"Sorry, I'm late. I was helping Jackie glue her kitchen chairs. It took longer than we expected." She holds out a hand and pulls off a strip of dried glue.

"That's fine. I'm reading a good book. Did Jackie want the meatloaf?"

"She gobbled it. I think she does go hungry part of the time. She spent all her money on tuition, books, and the apartment. She said the pork chop and muffin I took to her on Tuesday was supper and breakfast. Tonight she saved those cookies for in the morning."

"Why don't you invite her over for dinner on Friday night? You can put a roast in the crock-pot. Most everyone likes pot roast."

"Her mama's coming Friday afternoon."

"Invite them both. I'd like to meet your friend and her mother."

"I'll ask, but they may already have plans."

"Anyhow, cook the big roast. If we don't have company, we can eat the leftover in sandwiches."

That night Anna dreams of snakes and Jaeger chasing her in a green truck. She wakes with Mary shaking her. "Anna, what's wrong? What's wrong?"

Blinking and rubbing her eyes, she stares at Mary. "Was I having a bad dream?"

"A very bad dream. Your screams woke us all."

"I'm sorry. I'll close my door from now on. I hate that I woke you."

"Don't close your door on our account. It's all right. I'm truly glad it was only a dream. Go wash your face with a cool cloth. I'll get you and Carol some milk and crackers."

Carol, clutching a teddy bear, calls, "I want graham crackers." She runs after Mary.

Grabbing a robe Anna whispers, "I want Dad, Mom and Bart, the people who loved me most. I wish I'd never met Jaeger."

* * * * *

Bart places a Bible on his bed, sits on the side of the mattress with his head in his hands and prays. "Lord help me to remain strong. Don't let my anger for Jaeger destroy me and, please Lord, watch over Anna and keep her safe."

Chapter Seven

Friday morning Anna and Carol search the front yard with the metal detectors. They find a buckle and a plow point. Carol sits on the step and wipes sweat on her sleeve. "I thought we'd find gold."

"We may not find anything valuable, but I enjoyed looking. Did you?"

"I guess, but it's awful hot out here."

"Let's get some punch. Then I'll read you a story. We'll look more on a cooler day."

Listening to a pirate story, Carol falls asleep on the couch. Anna tucks a pillow under her head and covers her with a thin blanket. While the little girl naps, Anna sets frozen yeast rolls out to thaw and rise. She peels potatoes, carrots, and onions and adds them to the roasting pan.

Anna reads for an hour, mixes a chocolate cake in a plastic bowl so the electric mixer will not wake Carol, and then makes a salad. She is about to frost the cake when Carol calls, "Anna."

"Hey, sister-friend, you slept through lunch, so I ate it for you." She sits on the couch and wipes a sweaty curl from the little girl's forehead.

Carol grins. "What did you eat?"

"Cold meatloaf and cooked spinach."

"Yuck!" Giggles gurgle, like water in a mountain stream. "You're teasing. I'll wait for dinner." She grabs Anna in a tight hug and pulls her onto the couch.

Wrinkling her nose, Carol sniffs. "I smell cake."

"Chocolate cake—and I'm ready to frost it. Do you want to help?"

She nods. "Soon as I go to the bathroom. Wait for me."

"I'll wait, but don't forget to wash and dry your hands."

By the time Mary and the professor get home, Anna and Carol have the table set with china and glassware. Hot rolls are in a warming dish, and the roast is sliced and arranged on a platter with vegetables around it. "Mama, look! I helped Anna cook dinner."

"Oh, honey, it's beautiful, and it smells delicious." She waves to Anna and gives her an OK sign. "I need to go upstairs and slip on something casual. I'll be back to help."

Professor Dugan comes in the door, waves to Anna and runs up the stairs with Carol chasing and giggling. They return to the kitchen before the doorbell rings. Anna and Carol, holding hands, rush to answer. "Hello, Jackie and—"

The attractive, dark-haired woman holds out her hand. "I'm Betty Freeman, Jackie's mom."

After introductions, Anna grabs Jackie's arm. Help us serve the tea and lemonade and then we'll eat. Carol, find out what everyone wants to drink. I'll pour, and Jackie can serve."

Jackie and Anna head for the kitchen. Carol's loud voice follows. "Who wants lemonade? Anna let me squeeze real lemons."

Jackie looks around and whispers. "Wow. I didn't dream you lived in a place like this."

Anna, her face red from the hot kitchen, smiles. "I love it here. They couldn't be nicer if they were blood relatives."

Leaning close to the cake, Jackie inhales. "She's a good cook, too."

Anna grins and lifts two glasses of iced tea.

After the dishes are in the dishwasher, Jackie's mama stands looking out the sliding glass door while Mary and Anna serve cake and ice cream. "Your yard is beautiful. Do you sell the pecans? The trees are loaded."

"We haven't thought about selling them. We just moved here last December."

"Do you mind if I walk out and take a closer look at the trees?" She reaches to unlock the door.

"No! You can't." Carol puts her hand over the lock. "We have poison snakes. The terminator's got to come back and spray them."

Betty jerks her hand away as if the door were hot. "Poison snakes?"

Mary smiles. "Exterminator, Carol. Now go sit in your chair, if you want cake."

Carol, her eyes wide with worry, walks away. She knows she is not supposed to tell anyone about the snakes.

"We're close to a creek and wooded area. Next week, an exterminator is going to spray around the yard. Carol saw a snake in her playhouse and hasn't been in the backyard since."

Betty nods. "I don't blame her. I hate snakes, but I didn't know you could spray for them."

"Snakes come around to eat mice and insects—kill those and snakes leave." Mary picks up two plates. "Anna, this cake looks delicious. You're a wonderful cook."

After dessert, Jackie and her mother leave to go shopping. Carol watches until Betty's car rolls away, before she runs to Mary. "I didn't mean to tell, but she was gonna go in the backyard."

Mary hugs her. "It's all right, honey. That was an emergency."

Saturday, Anna goes to the library in search of more history. She finds interesting stories but no more about the rock house and old sea captain. Standing to gather books, she gets a glimpse of Jaeger and one of his friends coming in the front door. She runs into the women's restroom and locks herself in a stall.

Stepping onto the seat, she crouches, afraid to breathe. The outside door opens, and she hears one heavy step before the door swings shut. Anna cowers in the stall, her heart pounding until a group of giggling girls enter. Her legs ache when she steps down.

It is almost closing time before Anna leaves the library and goes to her car. She drives home, watching to make sure no one is following.

The professor is reading in the den. Anna taps the door facing. "Sir, may I talk to you about something that's troubling me?"

"Certainly; come in and have a seat."

She sits on the arm of a large chair and takes a deep breath. "I was at the library when I saw Jaeger and his friend come in. I don't think they saw me. I ran to the restroom and hid in a stall. I heard someone open the door, but no one came inside. I stayed in there a long time, but I never saw them again. Do you think I should sell my car and rent something unfamiliar to him? If he's got a buddy who's a crooked cop, they could check the new license plate and find out it's mine."

"Do you think he has a policeman friend?"

"I don't know, but I'm sure Jaeger wants me dead. Somehow, he must have discovered I'm going to the University."

"You'll lose a lot of money on your car. It's almost new, but a dealer won't give you a new price for it."

"I know, but I hate being afraid all the time."

"Do you have any idea what kind of car you want to rent?"

"Anything dependable."

He props his elbow on the chair arm, leans his chin on his fist and stares at the wall. "Let me think about this for a while." Before she can speak, he asks, "Do you have any pictures of Jaeger? I'd like to give one to the campus police and have them keep an eye out for him. He shouldn't be walking around the university campus."

"There are a few in my school annual. I can make a copy on your printer."

"Make the copy. I'll take it to the security office."

"I'll go find one."

"Anna, I want you to park your car inside the garage. I'll back mine onto the driveway, and until we think this through, I would rather you not drive your car on the weekends when Jaeger is not working. You can drive one of our vehicles to your Saturday class."

* * * * *

Monday morning a man calls and tells Anna he has a dumpster for the backyard.

"Drive around to the gate. Honk and I'll open it with the remote. You'll need to set the dumpster as close as you can to the old rock stable's entrance, but make sure you leave room to open the door."

"Lady, I'll need you to sign this delivery ticket."

"Drive around to the front of the house after you make the delivery."

"I can walk over to your back door."

"No, you'll have to drive around. That door's locked."

"If you say so, lady." There is a loud click on the phone, but she hears him muttering. "Rich people—everything's gotta be just so."

When he rings the doorbell, Anna scribbles *Mary Dugan* on the ticket.

Carol and Anna are eating lunch when the exterminator shows up with two boys. They clear out the hay within an hour, and the boys get in the truck. The old man puts on his mask, turns on the compressor and starts spraying gas inside the building. Anna opens the gate when he is ready to leave. "I hope his poison kills all those pests."

Anna is preparing the evening meal when Jackie follows Mary inside. "Hey, girlfriend, I finagled another dinner invitation."

Frowning, Anna tosses Jackie an apron. "I've got worries—a problem with my car. I need to leave it here until the professor gets time to check it out."

"What do you think is the problem?"

"All I know about cars is that you give them gas instead of grain. Help me set food on the table. We're having Carol's favorite—fried chicken."

Mary looks into the sunroom at eight forty-five. "Jackie, are you about ready for me to drive you home?"

She nods. "I can hardly stay awake."

Thursday afternoon, the exterminator returns with two boys. Anna opens the gate and goes to the stable with the sharp hoes. She hands one to each of the boys. "Take these with you. They're sharp enough to cut the head off a big snake."

The oldest boy laughs. "You're kidding. Grandpa guaranteed us the snakes were dead. We'll be going over the fence if we see a live one."

Facing the youngest, Anna winks. "Drag the dead ones out with the hoes. Professor Dugan wants you to put them in that metal trash can, there beside the oak tree." Anna walks to the house and gets the shovel Professor Dugan used to bury the first snakes. *I hope those guys don't know much about mambas.*

Anna glances at the upstairs window and waves to Carol. The exterminator goes into the building, but the boys lag behind. The old man calls, "Come on, boys, you're gonna have to clean out the basement. I can't do that with my bad back."

The boys ease up to the door; each one waits for the other to go first. The youngest boy shrugs and steps inside. The oldest slips in behind him. Anna hears the old man giving orders, boards cracking, something heavy landing with a thud, and a horrifying scream.

"Get me out! Get me out! Snakes!" The boy screams.

Anna runs in with her shovel. She can see where the rotten floor has collapsed. The old man, with a pained look on his face, clasps the front of his shirt and breathes quick and shallow. The largest boy stands back, stretching his neck to look into the hole, his hands shaking so hard that the hoe he holds dances against the floor.

Dropping her heavy shovel, Anna grabs the hoe from the terrified boy, steps to the opening, being careful not to step on darkened boards rotted from a leaking roof. She drops to her knees, pushing the blade over the edge. "Grab hold. I'll pull you out."

He grasps the hoe and tries to climb it. Slowly, it slips

through her hands—only a few more inches before it will slide away. The old man grabs the handle, above Anna's hands. The biggest boy wraps his arms around the man and pulls. The small boy climbs over them and runs outside.

Looking into the dark hole, Anna can see the bones of several skeletons protruding from faded blue uniforms. A long snake, unmoving, stretches over one set of pant legs. She backs away, breathing deeply.

Outside, the youngest boy walks around swinging his arms, mumbling, "Snakes and bones. Dead men, lots of them. Skulls were staring at me."

The oldest boy walks behind, pulling at the younger one's arm. "Danny, sit down. Sit and cool off. Those are stage props. Little brother, someone pulled a joke on us. They're plastic bones, and rubber snakes from some play. They didn't even look real. I bet the professor got them at the college."

"You're nuts! They're real! Real snakes! Real bones!"

The exterminator sits in his truck wiping sweat with a large blue handkerchief. Anna walks over to him. "Sir, bring your boys to the kitchen. I'll fix some lemonade. It's cooler in there."

Carol is downstairs before Anna opens the door. "Wash your hands, and fill five of those disposable cups with ice. They want lemonade."

Anna lifts the phone and dials the professor's number. "Sir, you need to come home as soon as possible. The exterminator came with two boys. One fell into the basement. He's not seriously hurt, only terrified. There are dead snakes and old skeletons down there." She hangs up the phone, grabs onto the counter for support and slides onto a chair.

"Carol, bring me a wet dishtowel from the sink."

"Anna, you look white." She hands her the towel. "Are you gonna faint?"

"Maybe not. This cloth helps." She sees the man and boys coming across the yard. "Carol, will you get three washcloths from the bathroom and wet them with cold water?"

Carol runs to the bathroom while Anna opens the door and points to the sunroom. "Have a seat in there while I pour the lemonade."

Carol returns with three dripping hand towels. "Give them to those guys so that they can wash their faces. It was hot in the stable."

Anna takes the full cups to the table. The exterminator and the boys are still washing their faces with the wet towels. "I called the professor. He'll be home soon."

The boy who fell in the hole is trying to wash the blood from his arms.

"Carol, go get the first-aid kit, please." Anna goes to the youngest boy. "Did you break any bones when you fell?"

He shakes his head. "Just scratched my arms. I don't think a snake bit me." He manages a weak grin.

She takes hold of one arm, and then the other, turning them to look at the scratches. Carol puts the first-aid kit on the table and backs away to the kitchen door. With a sterile gauze pad, Anna wipes away oozing blood and applies an antiseptic cream with a cotton ball before taping gauze pads over the scratches.

"I'm glad you didn't break any bones, but you'll probably have to get a tetanus shot unless you've received one recently."

"I don't need a shot. It's only scratches."

Anna refills their drink cups and goes to the kitchen for a package of individually wrapped fruit and nut bars. She hands

Carol one and dumps the remainder on a platter. "Help yourselves to these. Put the wrappers on the plate."

Anna hears Professor Dugans SUV. "Carol, will you get these guys some napkins? I'll be right back." She rushes to the front porch, closing the door behind her. In a few choppy sentences, she tells her boss what happened in the stable. "Do you want me to call the police?"

"I'll call the chief. I want to keep this as quiet as I can."

"Yes, if my name gets in the papers, Jaeger will—" She turns to open the door.

Carol runs toward her dad, but he points at her and says, "Go to your room and stay there while I talk business." She does as told.

Anna fills a glass with ice, pours lemonade and hands it to the professor. She sits in the dining room and takes another drink of her cola.

A faint rustle of movement occurs when Professor Dugan enters the sunroom. "Anna told me what happened. I can't tell you how glad I am that no one is seriously injured. However, I must insist that you take your grandson to the doctor, get those scratches dressed properly and get him a tetanus shot."

"Sir." The old man interrupts. "I know you'll have to call the law out here because of those skeletons, but can you just say I was spraying for bugs and scorpions." He clears his throat and takes a deep breath. "The poison I used is not legal in the states, but it's the only thing I know of to kill snakes on the spot."

"Can your grandsons be trusted not to tell it to their friends?"

"They won't tell. They're good boys, and they know my business is what keeps us in groceries."

"I'll agree if you and your boys won't mention anything about the girl who gave you the lemonade. She's in the process of getting a divorce from a brutal husband. If her name gets broadcast over the news media, he'll know exactly where to find her, and she's afraid for her life."

The boys shake their heads. "We won't mention her."

"You boys stay here and finish these fruit and nut bars while your grandpa goes with me to bury those critters. Then, no one should have a reason to mention snakes."

Anna jiggles the ice in her cup and sips the last bit of cola. *I wonder what kind of snakes are in the area where Bart's stationed? Unless they transferred him, it's not black mambas.*

*****

Bart goes into town with two of his friends for dinner. At the café, three girls approach and pull up chairs. Bart's friends order dinner and drinks for the girls. Bart eats and talks, but after dinner, he places money for a third of the bill on the table. "It was nice meeting you ladies. You're all pretty, but I know a girl in the US that's so beautiful she outshines every female I've ever met." He walks away.

Chapter Eight

With the last snake buried, Professor Dugan pays the exterminator in cash. "I'm adding an extra hundred to get your grandson a tetanus shot. Don't write me a receipt. I don't need a record of this transaction." Anna watches the big bills spread onto the table.

After the heavy steel gate slides closed behind the exterminator's truck, Professor Dugan picks up the phone and calls the Department of the Army. For days afterward, cars, trucks, and vans roll in and out of the backyard. The gate seems to moan louder each time it moves. Late one afternoon, a tall, gray-haired man with lots of metal on his uniform rings the bell to thank the Dugans for everything. He leaves, without fanfare.

Guards kept the press away from the house, until now, and all issued statements went out from headquarters. When the last military vehicle drives through the gate, Mary and Anna pull drapes and shades over every window. Reporters wait outside yelling questions and crowding close to cars leaving the garage. It is difficult to exit the driveway without hitting a journalist.

After the second day, Mary and Carol slip away at two in the morning and drive to visit Aunt Margaret. They drop Anna at Jackie's apartment, where she sleeps on the couch every night for a week.

Professor Dugan takes a room at a nearby hotel but returns the following Friday afternoon. Late Saturday morning, Mary, Carol, and Anna come home.

"Daddy, Daddy, I missed you."

"And I missed you." After a hugging session, the Dugans go to the kitchen where Anna is making chicken salad.

Mary takes a bag of chips from the cabinet, mixes a can of frozen fruit punch, and sets out paper plates and napkins. When they are sitting at the table, she says, "I've missed being at home with my family. Let's hold hands and give thanks for our blessings."

Carol cannot talk fast enough to tell her Daddy and Anna about the things she did while staying with Aunt Margaret.

"Eat your sandwich, Carol. You haven't given Anna or your daddy a chance to tell us about their week." Mary looks at Anna. "How was your week with Jackie?"

"She wanted to talk until long after midnight, every night. I need sleep."

Mary smiles. "How's school?"

"I like my teachers. Biology is hard, but Jackie's good at chemistry. She's my lab partner, and I think she can help if I have problems."

"Don't let yourself get behind. Get a tutor if you need one."

"I'll be all right. I'm home now, where I can rest and study."

"You do look tired. Maybe you should be taking vitamins. I keep multiples in the cabinet beside the sink. Help yourself to one every morning. I believe I have fewer colds when I take them."

"Thanks. Mom used to give me vitamins."

Mary places her hand on her husband's arm. "Charles, did you have a rough week?"

"Terrible—question, after question—one girl even asked if I helped remove uniforms from the . . . ."

"Daddy, what's uniforms?"

"Jackets." He looks at Mary. "Do we have anything for dessert, a little distraction?"

"Daddy, what's a distraction?"

He winks at Carol—Cookies, ice cream or maybe a brownie."

"I need to shop, but we do have brownie mix. If you clear the table, I'll stir it up."

Anna jumps to her feet. "I'll clear the table." She giggles. "I can't take a nap until after dessert."

Mary dumps a cup of pecans and a handful of dried cranberries into the mix. "This is sweet but healthy." She pours everyone a glass of milk.

The warm brownies are soft and gooey. Anna tries to resist taking seconds, but they are so good she cannot refuse.

"Can I rest with you, Anna? I missed you."

Before Anna can answer, Mary says, "No. Carol, you wouldn't sleep tonight if you take a nap. You can help Charles work in the front yard."

"Anna, can we use your treasure machines?"

"Sure, if your mama or daddy helps you."

The professor frowns at Carol. "If you and your mama will pull weeds from the flower beds, I'll help look for treasure."

Carol shakes her head. "There might be snakes. I'll watch from the porch."

Anna stretches out on the bed and closes her eyes. She jumps, blinking to focus when something touches her leg.

Carol, holding her doll, stands smiling. "I put my blanket over you so that you won't get cold."

"Thanks."

Feeling secure in the Dugan home, Anna closes her eyes to welcome sleep; again, she wakes with a start. Carol, asleep beside her, flops an arm across her face. Anna moves the plump little arm and closes her eyes. After several attempts to sleep, Anna gives up and goes to read a biology assignment.

* * * * *

Professor Dugan stands watching squirrels gather pecans that cover the lawn. "Mary, I don't have time to collect and shell pecans. What the squirrels don't get will ruin after the first hard freeze, but I don't know what to do with them."

"Let someone gather them."

"Who? I don't want strangers coming and going from our yard."

Anna clears her throat. "Sir, you could ask the exterminator if he and his grandsons want them. Pecans are quite expensive at the Farmers Market. They appear to be nice boys, and I bet they could use the extra money. I would gather them, but now I'm too busy with school. Midterm is coming up, and I have homework in every subject."

"Good idea. I'll call him." He hangs up the phone and makes an ok sign. "The old man said he'll be here late Friday afternoon with his grandsons."

Mary turns to Anna, "Do you mind staying with Carol all day on Friday? I need to work."

Friday morning, happy that she does not have class, Anna puts a brisket on to boil. "Carol, my mama used to fix brisket at least once a month. It takes a long time to cook, but they are good. After it boils tender, we'll rub it with brown sugar and mustard, and I'll bake it."

"Can I rub the sugar on?"

"Sure, if you won't lick your fingers."

Carol giggles. "Not while you're looking."

Carrots, potatoes, and onions are boiling, and the brisket is baking when Mary calls. "Anna, do you mind watching Carol tonight? Friends asked Charles and me to go out with them for dinner."

"I'll be glad to, but I cooked that big brisket. It's in the oven now."

"I would have called earlier, but Charles forgot to tell me until a few minutes ago. Maybe Jackie can come over."

"She went to her mama's for the weekend, but the old exterminator and his grandsons are in the backyard picking up pecans. Do you mind if I send some of it home with them? They commented on how good it smelled when I gave them water."

"That's an excellent idea. Thanks. I'll see you in the morning. Make sure the doors are locked and Carol brushes her teeth before she goes to bed."

"I'll make sure. Have a good time."

Anna sees the truck bed packed with containers, the western sky turning deep crimson, and the boys working at a frenzied pace. She wonders if they think this is their only chance to get the pecans. Carol skips along, holding to Anna's hand as they approach the old man. "Sir, you can come back tomorrow and Sunday afternoon to get the rest. It's about too dark to see out here."

"They want to sell them at the Farmers Market tomorrow."

"Next week then. Squirrels will get some, but there's still a lot of nuts on the trees."

"I've been having problems with my heart. I've got to go to the VA Hospital on Monday. Jim can drive, but he won't be old enough for a license until January. Until I get out of the hospital, they'll have to walk wherever they go."

In the fading light, she can see the worry on his face. "I hate to hear that. I hope everything goes well." Carol is jumping and yanking Anna's arm until she can hardly talk.

"Mrs. Dugan called to say they're going out to eat with friends. I made a big brisket with vegetables and hot rolls. She said we could share it with you if you like brisket. It would be a shame to waste it."

A big smile spreads across his wrinkled face. "A great shame. What do you say, boys? Think we could keep the brisket from ruining?"

They nod and lift buckets of pecans into the truck. Danny, the youngest, dusts his hands together. "I can sure eat a chunk of it. I forgot my lunch money this morning and haven't eaten a thing since breakfast. Where can I wash my hands?"

"Uh—there's a bathroom on the right as you go through the kitchen door."

He starts toward the house but stops. "I'll race you, Carol."

With a shriek, Carol is running beside him.

"Come inside when you get your tarp tied. I'll put the food on the table." Anna whispers to herself while walking away, "I hope Mary doesn't mind them eating here. I should have thought before I opened my mouth." She sets the large platter of meat and vegetables in the middle of the sunroom table. Carol puts out paper plates and fills five glasses with ice. Danny takes the pile of silverware from the bar and distributes it around the table, and Jim comes inside in time to pour the fruit punch.

"Mr., uh—I don't even know your last name."

"Tucker. Frank Tucker."

"Well, Mr. Tucker, you can sit at the end of the table. Everyone else, sit wherever you like. Mr. Tucker, do you want to say the blessing?"

"I can do that." He glances around the table. "Lord we thank you for this food and all your blessings. Amen."

Within twenty minutes, the meat and vegetables are gone. Danny and Jim reach for the last rolls. Anna pushes back her chair. "Does anyone want banana pudding?"

Danny straightens in his chair. "Banana pudding! We ate it when—Grandma made it." His smile vanishes and he looks down at his hands, resting on his lap.

The old man does not eat pudding but sits smiling as the boys scrape the bottom of the bowl. "My wife used to make brisket and banana pudding. You're a mighty fine cook for such a young girl. These boys haven't eaten this good since their grandma died. We certainly appreciate the meal. If not for your invitation, we would've probably opened a can of soup."

"Carol and I enjoy cooking, and we're glad we could share."

Danny opens the dishwasher and drops his silverware into the tray. Dropping his plate in the trashcan he says, "I like this kind of plate. At home, it's my job to wash dishes."

Anna smiles and picks up her plate and silverware. "Mr. Tucker, if you and the boys don't have a church home, we'd love for you to go with us on Sunday. Everyone is friendly, and you don't have to dress-up. Whatever you might wear to town or school is what most people wear. We're having a potluck after preaching. Women and girls prepare the meal. Men and boys don't bring food. It's the Center Street Church—not far from the college. The youth group will welcome Danny and Jim."

"I know where it is—across from the fire station. We might meet you there. I've wanted to get the boys in church."

"Sunday is a good day to start. Sunday school begins at nine-thirty, worship service at ten-thirty. You've never tasted more wonderful food, and I guarantee you'll feel welcome." She writes her cell phone number on a notepad and hands it to Jim. "Call me when you get near the church and I'll meet you at the door and walk with you and Danny to your classroom."

Before Danny goes out the door, Carol wraps her arms around him. He stands straight, hands at his side, a look of alarm on his face, and then he runs toward the truck. "He's my new friend," Carol says.

Anna calls after them, "See you at church." She stands in the open doorway watching until they are in the truck before pushing the remote to open the gate. They are almost through the opening when Anna feels panic. She pulls Carol inside, slams and locks the door before she pushes the button to close the gate.

She does not know why she experiences such fear but remembers the same sensation the day her parents died. "Carol, go sit at the top of the stairs, but don't turn on the hall light." Anna runs to check the front door lock. Wanting to look out at the street, she starts toward the front window but a hand seems to pull her back. Instead, she goes up the stairs, leaving on the kitchen light.

"Carol, let's play 'blind mice.' Have you ever played it?"

Blond curls jiggle as Carol shakes her head in the dim light. "How do you play?"

"We have to get ready for bed without turning on a light. Then we tell stories in the dark, instead of reading a book. The quietest one wins, but we have to brush our teeth and wash our face, hands and feet before we put our PJs on."

"What's the prize for winning?"

"You get to listen to three stories. If you lose, you have to tell me three stories."

"When do we start?"

"When I say go; afterward you can't say a word."

Carol nods.

"Go," Anna whispers and quickly walks to the window overlooking the front yard. Peeping from the side of the closed drape, she sees a black van pass under the streetlight and pause in front of the house. She grabs Carol's binoculars from a bookshelf underneath the window. The license plate letters are not clear, but the first three numbers look like 453. She licks her finger and traces the number on top of the bookshelf. A shot rings out and glass shatters downstairs.

"Carol, get under your bed and stay there until I tell you to come out." Anna grabs her cell phone and pushes 911. While waiting for the police to arrive, she punches in Mary's number and barely has time to explain before sirens and blue lights cause every dog for miles around to start howling.

"Anna! Anna!" Carol whispers, "Get under the bed with me."

"You can come out now. The police are coming to the door. Put your tee shirt on. Hurry, I need to open the door."

Holding hands, they rush down the stairs. Anna looks through the peephole before turning the deadbolt. A news van parks on the street as a police officer introduces himself and his partner. "Come-in. Hurry! I don't want to talk to reporters, or have my picture in the paper."

The officers step inside. "A lot of people would be waving to them."

"Not me. Last week, they were trying to take our pictures

and talk to us about those, those— " She looks at Carol. "Things found in the old stable."

"You mean the—"

"Yes, that's what I mean. We don't talk about it, you know, because of bad dreams."

He glances at Carol and nods. "Tell me what happened tonight."

Before Anna can speak, the Dugans come in the front door. Carol runs to her dad's arms and begins to tell him about the gunshot.

"Carol, you can tell me later. The policeman has questions to ask and papers to fill out."

* * * * *

Bart sits on his bunk reading his Bible while his friends prepare for another trip into town.

"Bart, I've never met a nicer, more generous guy or one so stubborn. You claim to be Christian, but you're in love with a married woman. God won't approve of that. He'll abandon you to a dark hole in Hell if you break up a marriage."

"I'll not break up a good marriage. Someday, God will give me a Christian woman to love. I'll wait."

"Man, do you think He'll just float her down and set her on a pedestal before you, saying, 'Here she is.'"

Bart grins, "Maybe, but unless He does, I'll get an engineering degree before I start looking."

His smile fades as they go out the door. He takes Anna's picture from his wallet and, again, prays for her safety. "God, I don't think I can be happy without Anna, knowing she is with someone as heartless as Jaeger. Please take care of her and keep her safe.

Chapter Nine

A large man, with sandy hair, wearing a white shirt and dark tie, comes inside. "I'm Detective Miller. I need you to tell me about the shooting."

She sighs. "I told everything to the other officer, and he wrote it down."

"Sometimes people remember additional information when they go over the story the second time."

"All right." She plops onto the couch and begins. "After the Tuckers left, I was afraid, for no apparent reason."

"Who are the Tuckers? You didn't mention them before, or that you felt afraid."

"A man and his grandsons. We gave them pecans from the backyard." She breathes deep and shrugs. "I can't explain feeling afraid. It simply happens sometimes—like the day my parents died."

"What happened to your parents?"

She props her elbow on the arm of the couch and lays her cheek in the palm of her hand. "Can I come to your office tomorrow and tell you all this. I woke early this morning and had a busy day. I'm so tired I can't think."

"I want you to come to my office tomorrow and review this after it's typed, but I need you to go over it once more while it's fresh in your mind. I won't keep you long."

"All right."

Professor Dugan stands. "While she's giving you the details again, I need to cover our broken window. I have a piece of plywood in the garage. I'll cut it to fit."

The detective barely looks up. "Sure. One of the officers can help lift it. You don't want a neighborhood cat coming in to explore while you're sleeping."

The Dugans, including Carol, go to the garage while Anna answers question after question. Before the detective closes his notebook, she has told him everything she knows about her parents' death, cruel things she knows about Jaeger, the wedding she barely remembers and her annulment. She even tells him about seeing Jaeger at the library.

Carol comes in slamming the garage door, and the detective stands. He has no good explanation for the shooting. "It was probably kids out for a joy ride. My guess is that they picked your house at random, but I'll check with the Faulkner County Sheriff regarding Jaeger, and your parents' accident."

When the Dugans come inside, the detective's attention turns to the window.

Anna has no comment for the detective, but she does not believe in his random theory. "Carol, let's go upstairs. It's bedtime."

"You don't have a bedtime. You're a grown-up."

"I do when I'm this tired. Come on—if I beat you getting ready for bed, you'll have to tell me three stories."

With a giggle, Carol races up the stairs, pulling off her tee shirt as she enters her bedroom. Before Anna gets her teeth brushed, her phone rings. With toothpaste in her mouth, she mumbles, "Hello."

"This is Danny. Listen and don't call me back. Are you all right?"

She mumbles, "We're fine." Holding the phone away from

her mouth, she spits toothpaste into the sink.

"We saw the black van and heard the shots. I got the last part of the license plate, but Jim told me to keep my mouth shut. I'll tell you if you won't say I gave it to you."

"Okay."

"It's RGL." The phone clicks.

Rinsing her mouth, she goes to the bookcase, licks a finger and traces RGL behind the 453, clearly visible in the dust on the dark oak wood. "Carol, you win. I have to say one more thing to the policeman, and then I'll come back and tell you three stories. Hop in bed and wait for me."

Rushing down the stairs, Anna hears the front door open. "Wait! I remembered the rest of the license plate. It's RGL."

The officer opens his notebook. "How did you manage to remember it?"

She shrugs. "It popped into my head. Roger's girl left—RGL."

Phone in his hand, the officer nods, steps outside, and pulls the door closed. Anna can hear him talking to someone.

Carol is still awake after listening to three stories. "Tell me more."

"Another night. I'm too sleepy. Carol, I have to get my rest so I can study tomorrow."

Anna crawls into bed, but questions will not allow her brain to slow. The annulment is complete. Jaeger knows he can't get a dime—even if she dies, he has no claim to anything—so why the stalking? He wanted the horses, car, the farm, money in the bank, but he did not care about her. She prays, "God, help me. Tell me what I should do. I'll lose my scholarship if I leave, but I may die if I don't, and what about little Carol and her parents?"

* * * * *

Sunday morning after Jim's call, Anna waits on the bottom church step for the boys. Again, she feels a sudden sensation of panic and steps behind a large green shrub. A black van with dark windows rolls along the street and through the parking lot. Squinting to see the license plate, she leans into the bush—982 CPL. She left her purse inside on a pew. Lacking pen and paper, she scribbles the number on the outside wall of the steps with a pencil size limb from the bush.

Anna dials the Police Department and asks for Detective Miller.

"Miller here."

"This is Anna, and a black van just cruised by my church and through the parking lot, but the plates are different—982 CPL."

"I'll run them. The other plates were stolen. Call again this afternoon."

She steps from behind the bush as the Tuckers' truck comes around a corner. Anna meets them in the parking lot.

Danny is all smiles, but Jim has a frown on his face. "Cheer up, Jim. You'll like it here."

Mr. Tucker goes into an adult classroom. Danny and Jim follow Anna to their classes. "I'm in the College group, but I'll see you in the auditorium. After preaching, we can follow our noses downstairs to the fellowship hall for the potluck."

Before going to class, Anna finds the deacon who usually makes announcements. "John, our guest today, Mr. Tucker, is going to the VA Hospital for tests on Monday. He's having heart problems. Please ask everyone to pray for him."

"Sure thing, Anna."

That afternoon Anna goes into her room and closes the door

before calling Detective Miller.

Abruptly, he begins, "Anna, I still think the shooting was a random prank. We have spoiled kids doing mischief in a town this size. I'll stay in touch." He is gone before she can say anything more.

Mary knocks on her door. "Anna, we're going to drive out to Beaver Lake and look for eagles. Do you want to go?"

"I'd love to, but it may take me all afternoon to get this algebra homework finished. Thanks for asking and have fun."

Their car is leaving the driveway when Jackie calls. "Hey, girl, I'm home from Mom's and it's so quiet around here that I can hardly stand it. Why don't you come over?"

"I can't, Jackie. I still have lots of homework. Just now, I opened my book."

"Ah, it's easy. You'll have the algebra finished in an hour, besides it's not due until Saturday. You have a week to do it. Come on over."

"I can't. I want to do those problems while I still remember the examples the teacher gave. Things were crazy around here this weekend. I have to study. I haven't read the biology chapters, and I'm so tired. I need to get in bed before ten tonight."

"Girl, you may have to go to a doctor and get sleeping pills. There are too many demons rattling around in your head. I enjoyed having you stay with me last week, and I'm glad you told me about your ex, those snakes, skeletons, and your—I've got to go. Someone's beating on my door. See you tomorrow morning."

The biology chapters hold Anna's attention, and she has no trouble working the algebra problems. She writes the last answer on her paper as the kitchen door opens.

Carol yells, "Anna, we're home. We saw two eagles." She bounds up the stairs. "You should've gone."

Holding her arms wide open, Anna says, "I finished all my homework."

Carol runs into those welcoming arms. "Now, you can eat tacos and burritos with us. Daddy bought a sack full."

* * * * *

Monday, after biology lab, Jackie insists on knowing everything about the shooting. Choosing words cautiously, Anna does not tell her most things she has kept from the Dugans. She trusts her new friend, but cannot bear to think about some problems and keeps pushing them to the back of her mind until they protest in the dark of night as nightmares.

She is glad to leave Jackie and the constant line of questions. Her head hurts from the stress. It will be nice to answer the simple queries of a child.

After three games of Candy Land and reading five books, they need something active. "Let's dance, Carol. You can be the princess. I'll be the prince, and we'll waltz like Cinderella at the ball."

"You'll have to teach me. I don't know how." She stands and holds her hands up for Anna to grasp.

Soft music fills the room. Carol, unable to reach Anna's shoulder with her left hand, takes hold of her sleeve. The lessons begin.

"Who taught you to dance, Anna?"

"My dad. Mom and I took turns dancing with him. We waltzed when I was your age. Later, he taught me lots of other dances, even the jitterbug."

"What's a jitterbug?"

"It's a fast dance. I'll teach you, but first you have to learn the waltz. Let's take our shoes off so it doesn't hurt when you step on my toes."

"Did you and your mom take off your shoes?"

"I did, at first. Mom was a good dancer; she never stepped on her partner's toes. Mom and dad were experts. They won contests. Tall trophies sat on our mantle. After I learned a few steps, Bart, a neighbor boy, asked if Mom and Dad would teach him."

"Was he your age?"

"A little older. He learned fast. At first, he danced with mom and then with me. By the time I was a teenager, we were good at most dances. He asked me to his Junior Prom so we could show off our dancing. Bart was strong enough to lift and twirl me in every direction. I don't think Cinderella could have enjoyed the ball more than I enjoyed Bart's prom."

Carol giggles. "Was he your boyfriend?"

She shakes her head. "No other kids lived near us, except Jaeger, and Mom didn't allow him to visit. He was mean to our animals. Bart and I rode horses, swam in the creek, played ball, and he helped when we built a tree house. I was a tomboy—he was my hero and my best friend."

"You're my best friend."

Anna hugs her. "And I'm lucky to have you as my friend."

"What happened to Bart?"

"He's in the Marines. I used to write to him, but I haven't got a letter in a long time."

"Oh! Anna, you stepped on me."

"Sorry. I was thinking about Bart instead of dancing."

Carol backs away to sit on the couch and rub her foot. "Did you give him this address?"

"I haven't given anyone this address, except my lawyer. No wonder I haven't got any mail."

"No wonder, you silly goose." Giggling, she runs when Anna tries to grab her.

"Goose, Mother Goose, I remember where I put his letter and address. Carol, where are those old books that I brought for you to read? His letter is in the Mother Goose book."

"Mama put that one on top of my bookshelf. She said she'll read it to me."

Anna runs up the stairs and grabs the book. Bart's letter is inside the front cover.

"Carol, let's sit in the sunroom and write Bart a letter. You can draw him some pretty pictures." She waves a blue envelope. "In this letter, he said he was missing trees, flowers, and butterflies like we have in Arkansas."

"Okay. I'll get my crayons."

Anna feels a mixture of emotions. It has been almost five months since she heard from Bart. "I bet Jaeger destroyed my letters. My head has been screwed up to let this much time pass without somehow getting in touch with my best friend."

She starts with an apology, tells him about the wedding she barely remembers, her escape from Jaeger, and continues until she fills ten pages with small handwriting. At the bottom she adds, "Please forgive me and write as soon as possible."

Carol has almost as many pages—with flowers, trees, butterflies, birds, snakes and even a crude picture of Danny. "Anna, my fingers are tired, can we stop now?"

"Oh, goodness, it's almost time for your parents. I haven't

started dinner. Leave the letters here on the table. We can finish them later. If I wash the lettuce, do you want to tear it into little salad pieces while I fry the fish and potatoes?"

"Sure, and I'll set the table."

On her way to class, Anna drops the letter at the post office. After class, she goes with Jackie to the library. Time ticks away, but she has not read a page. "Jackie, you're a good friend, and I enjoy talking to you, but I have to read these chapters. You and Carol are going to cause me to fail. At home, I can't study until after she's asleep, and I can't study here because you keep talking."

Jackie jumps up. "Sorry, I didn't know I was such a pest. I'll walk home and see you in the morning."

Anna grabs her arm. "Don't be unreasonable. There is no need to walk in the dark. Check out a book and read. When I finish this assignment, I'll drive you home."

Looking sullen, she walks away. Anna is halfway through a chapter when Jackie returns with a book. She sits and does not say a word until Anna is ready to leave.

"This is a good book. I hate to put it down."

Anna smiles. "I love to read, but I barely have time to get my homework. I need a place where I can be alone."

"Go to the library on Friday mornings—Mary's home until eleven. Go again on Saturday afternoon, after algebra. You need to work out a study schedule."

"How can I stick to a schedule?"

"I study every night after class and on Friday mornings."

"I've got bigger problems than study time. What will I do next semester?" She stops, takes a deep breath, and looks away.

"The Dugans will help you. I'm sure of it."

"I can't bring myself to tell them. I panic every time I think about the conversation. If Mom and Dad's house doesn't sell, I'll have no money. My scholarship only pays for tuition and books. I'll need more if I don't have a job. A lot more."

"Mary's a smart woman. She'll guess soon. I think you should tell her right away."

"Jackie, I shared my secret with you, but I'm afraid—afraid she'll tell me to get out."

"She won't kick you out. They're good Christian people. If she were going to toss you out, she would have done it after the shooting, or when she heard about Jaeger. She treats you better than my mom treats me." She shrugs. "But if you aren't ready, just tell her you have to study at the library on Friday and Saturday. Stay out of sight so she doesn't notice you're gaining weight."

"Jackie." Anna leans close and whispers. "I'm afraid—afraid I'll do something wrong. I don't know anything about taking care of a baby. The only kids I've taken care of were over three years old."

* * * * *

Bart is uneasy all week. His friends notice and ask if he needs to talk.

"I don't know what's wrong, just pray for me and while you are at it, pray for Anna."

He talks with the chaplain, but he does not ease Bart's worries. "Son, I think you need to forget about that girl and get on with your life."

"All I'm asking is for you to pray for her safety."

"I'll do that, and I'll pray for you as well."

Chapter Ten

Tuesday morning, at breakfast, Professor Dugan pulls four tickets from his suit pocket. "Carol do you still want to go to the rodeo?"

"Can we, Daddy?"

"We can. A friend gave me four tickets for Friday. Anna, will you be able to go with us?"

"I'd love to. I'll make sure I have my algebra homework finished before Friday night."

Carol bounces in her chair. "I'll wear my new boots and cowgirl clothes?"

Mary laughs. "This is why you've been saving them."

* * * * *

Carol and Anna place shirts and jeans on their beds and brush their boots.

Anna gets dressed while Carol bathes. Leaving the waist of her jeans unsnapped, she threads a western belt through the loops and skips a notch to buckle the thick leather. "I need to exercise more."

At the rodeo arena, the professor leads them to seats on the front row.

"Professor, the announcer is one of my daddy's old friends. So is Harry, the clown. Dad trained horses for them, and they've sat at our dinner table many times. If I get a chance, I'd like to say hello."

"Maybe, you can get around there during one of the breaks."

Carol is ecstatic. "Look, Anna, I could touch the horses if I stick my arm through the fence."

Anna frowns. "And if a horse came close it would break your arm before you could move. Don't ever stick your arm through the fence."

Before they can say more, cowgirls on beautiful horses race around the arena holding flags that snap and pop. Anna remembers the excitement of riding Polkadot in the Grand Entry. Carol jumps up to stand close to the fence. Anna kneels, putting a protective arm around her little friend. Watching the galloping horses, Anna gasps at the sight of familiar spots on her Appaloosa. "Polka! Mr. Prince didn't tell me he sold her."

A dark-haired girl leans forward while lashing the horse with a thick braided quirt. Polka's eyes display fear as she races ahead trying to escape the beating laid on her hip. Other girls hold leather quirts, but this girl shows no mercy. Anna has never used a whip on Polka—only tender urging.

The girl jerks the rein, causing the horse to turn too sharp at the end of the arena. Polka stumbles and tosses the girl from the saddle, but her left foot remains in the stirrup. Bouncing, and holding the saddle with one hand she tries to release her foot. Anna knows it is only a matter of seconds until the girl can no longer hang on.

Anna climbs the high fence and jumps into the arena, directly into the path of the frightened horse. Holding her arms out, she yells, "Whoa, Polka. Whoa!"

The crowd gasps.

The horse stops—inches in front of Anna. While trained rodeo workers release the girl, Anna holds onto the mare, talking gently and patting her head. Other riders, alerted to danger, stop and stand silent.

Unharmed, the girl curses Polkadot. "You freckled beast. I should beat you to death."

Anna grabs her arm. "If you hit her again, you'll be the one getting a beating. How did you get this horse?"

Jerking her arm free, the girl raises a hand as if to hit Anna. "My dad bought her. What's it to you?"

"She's mine. She was on consignment, but I have the option of signing the final agreement *if I approve of the buyer*." She shakes her head. "I haven't signed any papers."

"Good. I don't want such a clumsy horse. Take her away. I hope I never see her again. I'd have her shot if she were mine."

Other riders quietly leave. Anna climbs into the saddle and rides to the announcer's stand, leaving the hateful girl to walk away. Anna talks for a moment before riding Polkadot at a fast pace around the arena.

Outside the stadium, the dark haired girl approaches Anna. "I was upset and overly hasty. Thank you for stopping my horse. I'll take her now."

"No. You're not the kind of person I want to have my horse."

She grabs for the rein, but Anna steps in front of Polkadot, holding tight to the leather.

"Daddy paid for that horse. She's mine."

Harry, the clown, steps forward. "I heard you say you didn't want such a clumsy horse, to take it away, that you hope never to see her again, and you'd have her shot if she were yours. That animal will never perform for you as she does for Anna. She loves this horse, and the mare knows it. You need to have Daddy buy something else."

The dark-haired girl scowls and turns to walk away. "We'll

see what Daddy has to say about you stealing my horse."

Patting Polkadot's neck, Anna replies, "He'll get his money back."

Professor Dugan lays a hand on Anna's shoulder. "We can keep your horse in the fenced yard for a few days if you can get someone to haul her over."

The clown sticks out his hand to Professor Dugan. "I've got a trailer in the lot. I'll haul her for Anna, for free. That girl's daddy did several favors for me."

Professor Dugan rides with the clown, to give directions and open the gate. Anna and Carol climb into Mary's car. Arriving first, the girls linger in the sunroom waiting for the big steel gate to rumble open. Carol runs across the yard, pauses beside her playhouse to dance in place while she waits for Harry to back the trailer through the gate. Anna slows to a stop; holding her side, she leans against a pecan tree.

Stepping from the truck, Harry exclaims, "This is an excellent pasture. You must have over five acres here. With a few bales of good hay and some grain, you can keep a horse."

"My daughter wants one, but I thought we should have more pasture."

"If you give it hay and grain, you've got plenty of room." He bends and pulls a handful of grass. "You have a good stand of Bermuda. Horses love this." He drops the grass. "You won't have to feed hay until after frost, but are horses allowed in this neighborhood?"

"One per every five acres."

"Find a farmer who'll deliver hay, and you've got it made until that rich gal sics her dad's lawyer on you." Harry laughs and tugs at another handful of grass. "I'll testify for you if you need me. I'd hate to see a horrible gal like that get this gentle animal."

"The horse belongs to Anna. She's our daughter's sitter. She lost her parents in a car wreck, a few months ago. We help her all we can."

"I was at the funeral. They were good people." Seeing Anna leaning against the tree, Harry waves his hat. "Anna, let me know if you need me to testify for you, and if you want to sell Polka. I want the first chance to make an offer."

Standing straighter, while still holding her side, Anna shakes her head. "If Professor Dugan will let me keep Polka here and give Carol riding lessons, I won't sell her. Thank you for the offer to testify. I may need your help."

Harry nods. "Let me know if you do."

Carol is hanging on her daddy's arm as Harry leads Polka from the trailer. Anna turns and walks to the house. Mary stares at her as she enters the kitchen.

"What's wrong? You look pale. Sit at the table and let me get a cold cloth for your face."

Anna slides into a chair and leans on the dark wood. Mary brings the cloth and holds it to Anna's face. "When did you start feeling sick?"

"When I got out of the car my side was aching. Now, my low back, and my entire stomach hurts."

Gently, Mary rubs the cloth over Anna's forehead. "Do you think you could be pregnant?"

Anna draws in her breath. "I've been afraid to tell you. How did you guess?"

"You're sick every morning, and you've gained weight. Why were you reluctant to tell me?"

"I was afraid you wouldn't want me keeping Carol." Anna covers her face with her hands and sobs.

Mary puts her arm around Anna. "You're part of our family. Charles and I have already discussed possibilities, and we'll work out something so you can go to school."

With a swift gulp of air, Anna lifts her head. "You wouldn't mind a baby in the house?"

"Honey, Charles and I love children, but health problems prevent me from having more. We'd love for Carol to have a little playmate." She pats the cloth over Anna's brow. "I'm not ready to be called Grandma, but Aunt Mary sounds nice."

Forcing a smile, Anna squeezes her arms against her stomach. "I shouldn't have jumped from that fence to stop Polka." She stands, but leans on the table. "I need to get to the bathroom." Mary holds onto her as she slides to the floor.

The gate is closing behind the clown's trailer when Mary opens the back door. "Charles! Come quick! I need help!"

Carol runs inside before her daddy. "Anna! Anna! Mama, is she dead?" She grabs the wet cloth from the floor and dabs it against Anna's face. Tears overflow.

"She'll be okay. She fainted, but we need to take her to see a doctor."

It is two in the morning before the professor leaves the hospital with a very tired little girl. Carol can hardly keep her eyes open as they leave Anna's room. Mary leans back in the bedside recliner and reaches for a blanket. "Anna, call me if you need help. Usually, I'm a light sleeper."

"You should have gone home. I'll be fine. I wish the doctor would let me go. I don't know how I'll pay for this. I don't have any insurance. They'll have to wait until the antique shop or the farm sells."

"I think he'll let you go this morning. He said the surgery to remove a cyst is usually outpatient, but because it ruptured, he wants to get some strong antibiotics into your system."

Anna turns her head toward the window and sighs. "I have mixed emotions about this. I thought sure I was going to have a baby, but I worried about Jaeger's child growing up callous and evil." She pulls a blanket under her chin. "I need to trim my meals—this extra weight is fat."

Mary yawns and reaches to take hold of Anna's arm. "I'm glad your problem was only a cyst. You are too young to have the responsibility of a child. You need to finish your education and fall in love."

She squeezes Mary's hand. "I think that's what Mama would have said."

"I wish I could have met your parents."

"They were kind, and so much like you and Professor Dugan." Anna clutches the blanket and jerks her head toward Mary. "Jaeger has friends that rope and follow the rodeos; I hope none of them were at this one. I'm afraid, but I'm too weak to run."

"I think you'll be safe in here. I'll ask the nurse to take your name off the door, and I'll tell them not to give out any information about you."

"Thanks. I wish we could lock the door."

Mary stands and wipes a strand of red hair away from Anna's cheek. "You need to rest. Jaeger won't be out tonight. He works on Fridays; doesn't he?"

"Yes, and he probably drank several cans of beer before the rodeo."

"I'll bring us some hot cocoa. It should help you relax."

The next morning, a nurse takes hold of Anna's arm. "Hon, I need to get your vitals."

Anna turns her head. "What time is it? I thought you took them a few minutes ago."

"It's after six. The breakfast trays will be here soon. Do you want to see the newspaper? Your picture's on the front page."

"Oh! I hope you're kidding." Holding her side, she scoots up in bed.

"I'm not. It's in full color. No one could mistake such pretty red hair."

Mary stands. "Where can I get a paper?"

"You can read mine. Just return it to my station when you finish. I'll have no time to read until lunch."

Mary nods. "Thank you. I'll return it." She leaves the room behind the nurse.

Anna, still hooked to an IV, trembles. Staring at the needle, she picks at the tape. Slowly she pulls, grits her teeth and yanks. The tape is off. Without flinching, she pulls the needle out, drapes the cord over the pole, grabs a towel and her clothes from the cabinet, and steps into the bathroom. When Mary returns, Anna is dressed.

"Anna, it may be hours before the doctor comes in, and the nurse will have a fit when she discovers your IV needle is gone."

"Let her. I'm weak and dizzy from the shots and medicine they gave me, but I'm not staying here another night. I need to talk to Detective Miller. Do you mind if I call him on your cell phone?"

Mary hands her the newspaper. "Read the article first. It

doesn't give your name."

Anna gasps at the first sight of the color photo. "It doesn't have to. This newspaper goes out over the entire state, and his mama subscribes to it. They'll recognize me and Polka in a second." She closes her eyes and shivers. "What am I gonna do? I need someplace to hide, someplace where I won't put your family in danger."

Lifting the cell phone, she punches in the detective's number. After a brief explanation of why she is in the hospital and why her picture is in the paper, Anna asks Detective Miller to come to the hospital. She nibbles dry toast and pokes at the scrambled eggs on her tray until he arrives.

He closes the door behind him and pulls a chair close to the bed. "Anna, have you heard about the recent kidnappings in Arkansas, Oklahoma, and Texas?"

She squeezes her eyes tight and nods. "Yes, all young girls with red or blonde hair. Do you think Jaeger's involved?"

"We do. A deputy who helped search Jaeger's home for your property remembered seeing a bracelet in his sister's playhouse. He thinks it is identical to one worn by one of the kidnapped girls. He said you told him it was not yours."

"I remember him asking. It was a beautiful bracelet and looked expensive."

"Jaeger and his parents are prime suspects. They may have murdered a game warden who discovered where they were hiding a couple of the girls. They bonded out of jail but are closely watched."

"Then it wasn't just nightmares."

"What do you mean? Is there something you haven't told us?"

*****

Shouting and laughing, Bart rips open the overstuffed envelope from Anna. His friends crowd around and look at Carol's drawing as Bart reads.

"Thank you, God. Thank you. You answered my prayers."

"Tell us your news, man."

"Anna got an annulment. Jaeger drugged her and forced her into marriage. Now, she's going to college and waiting for me to come home." He picks up his Bible and holds it in trembling hands. "Thank you, God, for helping Anna and me."

Chapter Eleven

Anna takes a deep breath and exhales quickly. "Since leaving Jaeger, I've kept busy every waking minute, studying, watching Carol, and going to class. I never have time to ponder what happened while I was with Jaeger, and I don't want to remember. I want to forget everything about him, but at night, I keep having nightmares. I wake up with my heart racing; sometimes I'm screaming."

Mary nods. "Twice I went in to calm her."

"Tell me about them." The detective clicks on a pocket recorder.

"First I want to say, I'm convinced Jaeger drugged me. In my right mind, I would never have married him. I didn't even like him. I was polite, and I left myself vulnerable."

"Criminals take advantage of courteous people. Tell me about your nightmares and fear."

I can't remember much of what went on; I'm sure he kept me drugged, but I had rope burns on my wrists and ankles when I escaped. She shivers and rubs her wrists. "I'll try to put things in a timeline of how, I think, they happened."

He nods. "Good."

She wrings her hands and bites her lip. "The last week before Dad died, he was coming from the barn one morning when I came home from my babysitting job. He stopped at the porch and said, 'Listen, Anna.' We stood silent for a few minutes.

"I said, 'Dad, it sounds like someone screaming.'"

"I know. I've been hearing it since I woke this morning. I've heard people say a panther's cry is similar to a woman's scream, but this is too real. I'm going to report it to the sheriff and game warden. It's bad either way. Our mares will be dropping foals any day. We can't have a big cat hanging around."

"Do you know if he reported the screams?"

She nods. "While I was getting ready for school, he called the game warden. I don't know about the sheriff. I heard him telling Mom that he'd noticed Jaeger's truck going into the woods every day. Jaeger's dad has a small barn over there. One day when Dad was looking for a colt with the binoculars, he spotted padlocks on the barn's doors. Mom said Jaeger was probably keeping his drugs locked up."

"What did your dad say about the drugs?"

"He said he was worried that Jaeger was into something deep. He told her he'd heard a helicopter land over in that direction once or twice a month before dawn."

"Did he think Jaeger was dealing drugs?"

"I don't know. I was in a rush to get to school, meet some friends and collect my cap and gown for graduation. I never heard more of the conversation, but soon afterward, the news media reported a game warden was missing. Dad and Mom died the day they planned to talk to the sheriff about that. I don't know if they spoke to him before the wreck or not."

"Did you tell any of this to the sheriff?"

"No. I was terribly confused following the accident, especially after Jaeger came around. I'm sure he was doctoring my drinks—starting that evening he came to the antique shop. I was his prisoner from that day until I got away. Once I escaped, I tried not to think about him, and I was afraid someone in the sheriff's department might be friends with him."

"The FBI is involved because of those missing girls. They'll probably be calling on you today."

"They need to get over here right away. I want to leave—soon. Jaeger and his friends will try to kill me, and I don't want to put the Dugans in more danger."

"You can't leave. You're a witness."

"What I know will get me killed."

"I'll ask the FBI officer if they can put an around-the-clock guard on you."

Anna taps her fingers on the tray table. "I hate to waste a semester, and my scholarship because of him. I'm eighteen now—am I old enough to get a permit to carry a gun? I'm a good shot with a rifle and a pistol."

The officer frowns. "You couldn't take it on campus."

Anna looks at Mary. "I'm sorry about causing trouble for your family."

Someone drops a tray in the hall. Anna jumps and grits her teeth. "I hate this noisy place. Mary, will they let me charge this bill? I can't pay, and every hour they keep me is adding to the cost."

"They can't keep you against your will. They'll have to release you."

"Then let's go."

"The doctor will need to sign your release, but you have to go home with me. You'll be safer there than anywhere. Charles has taken Carol to her Aunt Margaret's. She'll stay there for a week until you feel better. Charles will notify the teachers of your illness; Jackie can bring your homework assignments, and return your work until you're well enough to go."

"I should rent a room somewhere and not put you in danger."

Mary pats Anna's hand. "I'm not afraid and Carol is safe at Margaret's. If it makes you feel more secure, you can strap a pistol on your hip during the day when Charles and I are at work."

"It will. I don't want to become someone's slave in South America."

Detective Miller clicks the recorder. "What makes you say South America? Did you hear something else—something you haven't told me about?"

"Yes, the night he put that awful bruise on my face he said something like, 'You'll get worse in South America' and how could I have forgotten what Jaeger's dad said?"

The detective holds the recorder close to her face. "What did he say?"

"One night I went to bed while Jaeger was watching TV. I woke, hearing his dad's loud cursing on the front porch. He said, 'Jaeger, find yourself a dark-haired girl. You know we can get more for blonds and redheads in South America.'"

Detective Miller leans closer with the recorder.

"Jaeger laughed as if it were a joke, and said, 'Give me time; I want all the trimmings.'"

Detective Miller clicks the recorder off. "We'll need more proof to put them away."

Anna shakes her head. "Yes, Jaeger will deny it. I wish you could find those girls and the game warden."

"We found him about a half mile downstream in the creek that runs behind Jaeger's home—lodged in a tree root below the water's surface with a bullet in his head. We found where the helicopter landed, footprints in the mud and a piece of cloth from one girl's dress. This is a big operation; Jaeger and his daddy are only a small link in the chain."

A nurse enters the room. "Sir, will you step out in the hall for a few minutes."

"Anna, I'll wait by the door."

"Young lady, you should not have removed that IV needle. The hospital will not be responsible if you get an infection."

The doctor comes in, checks her chart, looks at her arm and the incision, signs the release papers, tells her to come see him in his office the following week, and leaves quickly.

"Mary, they didn't say a thing about the bill. Let's leave."

"Anna, you need a wheelchair. I'll get one from the desk if they don't bring one soon and I'll tell Detective Miller to send the FBI officers to our house."

* * * * *

In her bedroom, at the Dugan home, Anna snuggles under a blanket and is soon asleep. She wakes to the scent of roast chicken and chocolate cake. "Thank you, God, for giving me a second loving family."

Weak from surgery, she slides onto the overstuffed chair beside her bed and opens a textbook. She learned early in life to take advantage of time. "If I stay alive, I have to graduate."

Anna wants to help Mary in the kitchen but feels faint when she stands. Left downstairs on the kitchen counter, her cell phone rings several times. Mary answers it, but Anna cannot hear the conversation. She reasons that it is probably Jackie, wondering why she did not show up for Algebra class.

Late in the afternoon, Professor Dugan returns from taking Carol to her Aunt Margaret. His words resonating—Anna hears him say, "Carol didn't want to stay with Margaret. She thought Anna might need her to help next week, and she made me give my word to keep plenty of feed and water out for Polka. She's looking forward to learning about horses."

"Do you want to feed the horse while I put dinner on the table? It'll be ready in ten minutes."

"I'll be ready. I stopped at the feed store for grain, and a bag of apples."

"You'll have Polka as spoiled as Carol."

"I enjoy spoiling my girls."

The sliding door closes. Anna hears silverware and plates shuffling. The chicken smells delicious, and she can almost taste the browned potatoes and carrots.

Mary, at the bottom of the stairs, calls, "Anna, do you feel like coming down to eat? If not, I'll bring you a tray."

"I'll come down. I need to move about."

At the kitchen door, Professor Dugan stomps his feet on the mat before stepping inside. "How are you doing, Anna? You gave us a scare last night, especially Carol."

"I'm weak and my side is sore but thankful for this family. I miss Carol."

"Me too, but busy days pass quickly."

After the blessing, Mary says, "Jackie called. I hope you don't mind me answering your phone. I told her you were resting. She said she'll copy her notes for you, and tell you all the assignments."

"Thank you. I'd still be on the phone. Jackie likes to talk."

Professor Dugan clears his throat. "I stopped by the storage unit and picked up your saddle. I heard you wishing for it. It's a good thing you gave me a key and put my name on the rental agreement; otherwise, you'd have to go get it."

"Thank you. I'm so glad you thought of it. I was dreading that long drive down the mountain."

"I'll store it in the garage until I can get a small building built with a tack and feed room. I'd like to burn that old barn. It's a wonder Danny didn't break a leg when he fell through the rotten floor."

Anna nods and places her fork on her plate. "I've been wondering about Mr. Tucker. Do you know what the VA doctor told him about his heart?"

"No, I should have called. I'll call after dessert."

Anna sits at the table covering the leftovers with plastic wrap while Mary loads the dishwasher. The professor comes from the sunroom, still holding his cell phone. "Mr. Tucker will have surgery on Monday morning. Mary, do you mind if those boys spend a few nights over here? I'll pick them up at the hospital and bring home pizza, tacos, or something for dinner, and drive them to school on Tuesday. We'll take the rest of the week, one day at a time."

"I don't mind. They can sleep in Carol's room."

He nods and starts pushing numbers on his phone. "I'll notify the preacher and care groups to pray for him."

Anna does not comment, but cannot help feeling uneasy about the boys spending the night in Carol's room. She would not mind Danny, but there is something unsettling about Jim. She remembers Danny telling her that he got the last part of that license plate number, but Jim told him to keep his mouth shut. Was he afraid to get involved? Or could it be something worse?

That night, in bed, Anna keeps thinking about Jim, and the many bad things some teenage boys get into—especially boys like Jim with no spending money and no way to earn it legally. She gets up and dials Jackie on her cell. After telling her about the rodeo, Polka, and the surgery, she asks Jackie if she will do her a big favor.

"Sure, I'll do most anything you ask, short of murder."

"I can't miss a whole week of school. Will you let me stay in your apartment, and drive us to and from school?"

"Sure, but did you get your car fixed? I can't drive Professor Dugans old truck."

"My car's okay. You can drive it."

"I hate to ask, but what about food? I can barely afford soup and crackers for myself."

"I wouldn't stick you with a food bill. I'll pay for two-thirds if we eat balanced meals."

"I'll push you into the grocery store and you can buy whatever you want, as long as my share is no more than forty dollars."

Professor Dugan opposes the idea of Jackie driving Anna's car. "Make a list of what you and Jackie want to eat; I'll go get it and take it to her apartment. It might not be so dangerous when Jaeger's working, but stay inside when you can. Jaeger is not the only one involved in this."

Anna goes over the ads for a local market, creates a menu for the week, and makes a grocery list including sandwich meat for lunch. She counts out six, twenty-dollar bills and hands them to Professor Dugan. "If the total is more, put something back. This is almost all my cash."

When she talks with Detective Miller, he agrees with Professor Dugan. "Jackie should not take your car from the garage. Driving your red Mustang is like waving a target. I wish you could stay at home until the trial is over, but I know you have to keep up with school."

Monday morning, at six-thirty, the Dugans and Anna are taking their plates to the sunroom for breakfast when a young FBI man rings the doorbell. After asking for identification, Professor Dugan invites him to join them. He refuses breakfast but takes a cup of black coffee.

Entering the sunroom, he nods to Mary and Anna. "I'm Detective Joseph McGraw. Just call me Joe." He nods again to Anna. "You're even prettier than the pictures in my file. I see why you are worth a lot of money in South America."

Scrambled eggs fall and her fork clatters against the plate. Quickly, she clasps trembling hands in her lap.

"My boss wouldn't agree with my guarding you around the clock, but I'll drive you to class this morning if you want."

"Thanks, but Professor Dugan will drive me, and I'll stay on campus until he leaves work each afternoon. I have large assignments in my evening courses, so I don't have to attend those until the homework is due."

Monday evening Mary calls to let Anna know that Mr. Tucker's surgery went well. The preacher will take the boys home on Friday afternoon, with food from the churchwomen.

"Good! I need to be where I can study." Jackie walks into the room. Quickly, Anna asks, "Will Carol come home this weekend?"

Friday, Anna is barely inside the Dugan home when two FBI agents arrive, follow her into the den and close the door. She answers question after question, most of which she has already answered more than once. They cannot understand why she decided to go to Jackie's apartment after hearing about Jim and

Danny coming to stay in Carol's room. "This is the safest place for you."

Anna takes a deep breath and speaks softly, "I knew I'd feel uncomfortable living so close to two boys and sharing a bathroom with them. My bedroom door doesn't have a lock. I'm an only child, no brothers or cousins, and not much older than Jim. Something about him makes me nervous. I don't trust him."

Saturday afternoon, the two FBI agents return to tell Anna and the Dugans that the police picked up the boys involved in the shooting. They were teens, one confessed to smoking marijuana. Only the driver knew where the weed came from, but he knew plenty. His dad was dealing drugs. With his mother's lawyer, the boy plea-bargained with everything the inquisitive teen overheard—the site of a warehouse, names of growers, buyers, sellers, and details that led to the location of two kidnapped girls.

Jim's name was on the list of sellers. Anna shakes her head as she learns of Jim's betrayal. A chill runs through her at hearing he is in Mr. Tucker's custody until trial.

"What about Jaeger? He is the guy holding the most vengeance for me."

"He's under investigation. We can't tell you more. If anyone asks—family, friends, neighbors—tell them all this involved teenage boys out on a marijuana smoking joy ride. We have to keep the rest quiet to rescue other girls. Two are still missing."

* * * * *

Bart tells the Chaplain his good news about Anna's annulment.

"Son, we shouldn't rejoice at the separation of what God joined."

"Sir, you don't understand, Jaeger drugged and forced her into marriage."

"Maybe, but they were joined in matrimony."

Bart turns on his heel and yells, "God didn't join them. She was kidnapped."

Chapter Twelve

Anna sits on the top step of Carol's playhouse brushing tangles from Polka's long tail. "Girl, remember when I used to brush you every day and keep your hooves buffed to a soft shine. I know Mr. Prince didn't have time to give you such special attention, but Carol and I will take care of you. Carol will love you as much as I do."

"Yes, I'm sure she will."

Anna jumps at the sound of Mary's voice.

"Carol is excited about learning to ride, and you are the perfect teacher. This letter came to you, from Bart Grayson. With all the turmoil, we didn't check the mailbox until a short time ago. I don't remember hearing his name. Do you think the detectives should check it?"

"No. Bart's an old friend—we were kids together. I wrote to him last week." She takes the letter, follows Mary to the house and opens the envelope inside the warm sunroom.

Dearest Anna,

I can't express my sorrow over the loss of your parents. They were family to me. I couldn't be there for the funeral; the Marines wouldn't give me leave. I stared into the darkness many nights wondering about you. Aunt Alice wrote that you married Jaeger. I couldn't help crying when I read her letter—my first tears since I was eleven, and you fell out of the sycamore tree and broke your arm. You've always been special to me, and I knew you would have a hard life with him. My friends thought I'd received a 'Dear John letter.' They cheered for me when I read your letter saying you got an annulment.

I'm sure Jaeger put drugs in your cola. Aunt Alice said you seemed in a daze at the wedding. She thought you were still in shock over the death of your parents.

I will get out of the Marines early if I join the Reserve. I plan to enroll at the University of Arkansas. With the classes taken while in the Marines, I'll have three years to complete for my bachelor's degree. We may graduate together. I look forward to seeing you again. You are more fun than anyone I've ever known.

Take care until I get there to guard your back.

I love the pictures Carol sent. They remind me of summers we spent together—swimming in the creek, wildflowers, butterflies, green trees—especially the tree house. I taped them to my wall. My friends enjoy them, too.

Love always,

Bart

She reads the letter three times before putting it in the envelope. Mary brings a glass of lemonade and places it on a coaster. "Bart must be a special guy. I've never noticed such a far-away look in your eyes before."

Sensing her face getting hot, Anna grins. "He is special, like a brother, not a boyfriend. He'll probably get out of the military in May. Here, you can read it. It's not a love letter." She pushes the paper across the table.

Mary reads, smiles and returns the letter. "He sounds like a keeper to me. Don't be too hasty and let him get away."

Carol bounces into the room. "Mama, I'm home." She hugs Mary and runs to Anna. "I'm glad you're back. Do you have a big scar? Does your side still hurt? Can you teach me to ride Polka?"

"The doctor said the scar will hardly show after a year, and my side only hurts when I move. You'll have to take care of me next week. After that, maybe you can ride."

"But I can't cook."

"We'll eat sandwiches and fruit. I have three big tests next week, and I have to study. If you play quietly while I study, I'll teach you to ride after I pass my tests."

She frowns. "It'll be hard, but I can do it for a week."

Carol keeps her promise not to bother Anna. She is entertained with brushing and leading Polka around the backyard.

Saturday morning, after the Algebra test, Anna is tired but elated. "Jackie, we could get shot if we go out to celebrate. Maybe, Mary will let us bake cookies."

"I would rather have pot roast. The groceries you bought ran out on Wednesday. I didn't want to take the time to shop and cook, so I ate peanut butter or cheese sandwiches."

"Pot roast takes a long time to thaw and cook, but I bet Mary has something good planned for lunch. I'm sure she'll welcome you. Although, keep in mind that Carol is planning on riding Polka this afternoon."

"Sounds like fun. Do you think she'll give me a turn?"

Anna giggles. "She can't ride all afternoon without stopping for a snack. Do you know how to ride?"

Jackie shrugs. "I've never tried. I figure if the horse is gentle, all I'll have to do is hold on."

"That's mostly it, but there are a few things you need to know."

At Carol's request, Mary prepares fried chicken; hot biscuits, mashed potatoes, green salad, and baked beans. The girls do not waste time getting to the table.

After stuffing themselves, Carol rushes them to the backyard. Jackie helps Carol on and off the horse and leads it around the yard. Anna sits in a chair and gives instructions.

"Anna, can I make her run?" Carol asks.

"No. Not until you've been riding at least two weeks."

"Two weeks is a long time."

Anna grins. "You have a lot to learn. You have to understand how to get on and off by yourself without falling, know how to brush and feed her, and learn what's safe for you and Polka."

"I already know how to feed her. I watched Daddy."

"Did you know that if you give her too much feed, you could kill her?"

"Why?"

"Because horses will keep eating until they get foundered. Horses get a sickness from overeating. They can die from it. So, never feed her more than you're supposed to. I'll show you how much."

Carol and Jackie ride and listen to Anna's instructions until all three are tired and chilled in the November wind.

"Anna can we stop for hot chocolate?"

"First you need to rub Polka with a dry towel and put a

horse blanket on her. You've worked her a long time. If you don't dry her off and put a blanket on her, this cold wind could make her sick."

Jackie rubs Polka's face and neck, Carol stands on the playhouse steps and rubs her side. Carol giggles. "Jackie, you have to dry her behind. She might kick me."

Anna stands. "I'll do that while you watch. You must be careful and never do anything to frighten a horse, or she might kick. Polka is extra gentle, but you still need caution. Once, Daddy accidentally dropped a metal bucket behind a gentle horse. It kicked the bucket across the barn. Daddy was off to one side, or it might have broken his leg. Horses get frightened the same as humans."

Mary has hot chocolate and oatmeal cookies on the table when the girls come inside.

Anna picks up a cookie and takes a bite. "Carol, Bart liked the pictures you drew for him. He hung them over his bunk. Next week, do you want to help make cookies for him and his Marine friends?"

Her mouth full, she nods.

That night, Anna does not have nightmares. She dreams of dancing with Bart and wakes with Mary's words echoing, "He sounds like a keeper. Don't let him get away."

Bart and his friends send letters to Carol thanking her for cookies—she returns crayon pictures—Anna gets long letters from Bart.

Detective Miller calls to tell Anna that two kidnapped girls were found alive in Stone County, and the judge ordered Jaeger held over for trial without bond since they identified him as one of the captors. "Anna, you'll have to testify at the trial, but

Jaeger's where he can't harm you."

At the news, Professor Dugan walks around the kitchen, slamming a fist into his hand; a frown shrouds his face. "Anna, you can't take a gun on campus, but you can keep it with you in our home. I'm afraid you're in danger from that drug gang. The FBI should guard you, but since they won't, you'll have to be extremely careful."

"If you want, I'll move out. I don't want to make your home unsafe."

Professor Dugan turns to face her. "I don't think we are in danger, only you. This may go on for a long time." His voice trails. "Next semester, try to get as many on-line classes as you can. Don't take any night classes. I'll talk to your counselor and get him working on your schedule. When you get a chance, stop in and talk to him."

Carol hears the conversation and asks questions.

Professor Dugan frowns and sighs. "Carol, you're young, but you have to know that Anna's in danger. She must tell in court what she knows about some bad men. They don't want her to tell the judge, so they might try to harm her. If she tells you to hide or to be quiet, you must do exactly what she says."

Her brow wrinkles; she swipes the back of one hand across her eyes and asks, "Won't the detective come with his gun to protect her?"

"No, but Anna can wear a gun on her hip while here at home. Remember, hide and don't make a sound if Anna tells you, or if you see or hear strangers trying to get inside."

Seeing her little friend in distress brings tears to Anna's eyes. She goes to sit on the playhouse steps. Polka comes to nuzzle her hand but finds no apple or sugar cube.

Sitting there rubbing Polka's head, Anna notices her bedroom window is at least six feet from the outside wall. From inside it is less than two feet from the inside wall. "How strange. The old sea captain may have built a secret room or staircase in there."

She rushes upstairs to her room and runs her hands over the wall. It seems solid when she taps it with her fist. In Carol's room, there are two large wallpapered panels where Mary has hung pictures of zoo animals. Each panel covers almost half of the wall. She taps on one; it sounds solid. The second one sounds hollow. She removes the pictures and places them on Carol's bed before pushing sideways on the panel with the palms of her hands. It will not slide, but it gives when she pushes in.

Rushing downstairs, holding her side, she asks, "Professor, where's Carol?"

Frowning, he points toward the sliding glass door. "In the yard with Mary."

"I think I've found a secret panel in her bedroom, but I couldn't slide it over."

He dashes up the stairs. Anna gets a wide, flat-head screwdriver and a sturdy spatula from a kitchen drawer and follows. Together, they press and pull on the plate until it slides sideways. A dusty stairwell leads down to two doors—one on the outside wall, one to the inside. "My word, Anna, I never dreamed this house could have a secret stairwell. It's deep, well past the first floor. It must lead to a cellar." He takes a step.

"Wait! Let me go to the garage and get those sharp hoes. In case we find a snake." She is on her way before he can comment.

With weapons in hand, and a flashlight she grabbed from a

kitchen drawer, they inch down the steps. He opens the door that goes underneath the house. A large room and several dusty cots are before them. "This must be servant's quarters. Now, we have a place to go if a tornado comes in this direction. Get your hoe ready before I open the outside door."

Anna breathes deeply. "I'm ready."

The door is stuck. He pushes hard and slams his shoulder against it before it will budge. The bottom drags and the top squeaks. Little by little, it opens into a long rock hallway.

She hands him the flashlight and peeps around his shoulder. "I bet it leads to the stable. Do you think it's cold enough for snakes to hibernate?"

"I think so. It was thirty-eight degrees last night, but it seems warm in here. Let's go slow and look close."

"Oh, the smell, it's horrible. Something is dead. Wait! Most disturbed snakes give off a rotten egg scent. We need some of Mr. Tuckers poison."

"Look, Anna. There's a heavy screen between that room and us. The odor is coming from in there." He shines his light through the screen. Decaying snakes lay scattered inside, what looks like, a prison cell.

"The poison must have made them sick before they crawled in there to die."

"I don't see any more blue uniforms and skeletons. I'd hate to call the feds out again. I wonder if they found their way in here."

"Professor, can we go now and close this off. If Carol finds out about this tunnel, you'll have a hard time getting her to sleep in her room."

"You're right. We'll seal it until I can think this over and decide what to do."

"I wish Mr. Tucker could fill this area full of poison."

"I agree. When we get freezing weather, I'll open the outside doors to let in the cold overnight; then you and I can clean out the barn. We'll call Tucker back if we see any signs of live snakes."

"Polka's got to have some shelter before it gets much colder."

"I'll get bids on having a small barn built, but I was waiting until you hear something from that girl's dad. If he should take the case to court and win, I'd have an empty barn in my yard."

"I called Mr. Prince. He returned the deposit and hasn't heard anything more. He has a receipt that states the sale is contingent on my approval."

"Good enough. I'll get to work on the barn." They slide the panel into place and hang the zoo pictures on Carol's wall. Anna is in her room reading when Carol comes inside.

"Mama led Polka while I rode around the yard."

Anna smiles. "Did Mary ride?"

Carol shakes her head. "She said you need to give her a lesson first."

"During Christmas vacation I'll devote most of my time to riding lessons. I'll be well enough to ride by then."

"Carol." Mary's voice is demanding. "Come downstairs. Anna needs to study."

Carol is better about being quiet so Anna can study, but after the last test of the semester, she dances, jumps, and squeals. "Anna, we can play for two weeks."

"We'll play and ride Polka, but I have some shopping to do, and I promised your daddy to help clean out the old barn. Soon, we'll have snow, and Polka has to have a warm, dry place to rest when she's tired and cold."

"I heard Daddy tell Mama that a man's coming tomorrow to build a new barn. He said Danny's brother works for the man. I wish Danny could come with them."

"Polka needs a warm shelter. I think about her when the wind blows cold." Anna answers calmly, but she wants to scream, "Not Jim! Professor Dugan, why Jim?"

Things are more peaceful with Jaeger in jail, yet Anna worries about the trial coming up in January. Campus security kept a close eye on Anna, but she is more and more afraid as December ticks away, thinking the drug gang will never let her testify.

Placing her textbooks on a shelf, she sighs. Jackie talks too much, but up here, she's Anna's only friend, except for the Dugans. She wishes she could go home to her parents, like Jackie, during the holidays.

*****

Sunday morning, Bart sits on his bunk trying to decide if he should go to church. He is still angry with the Chaplain for his accusation. He says a prayer, picks up his Bible and walks toward the meeting hall. The sermon is about compassion and forgiveness.

After lunch, Bart sits alone in his room to write Anna.

Chapter Thirteen

Saturday morning the temperature is three degrees above freezing and equally cold inside the old barn; the doors remained open all night. With her sharp hoe standing against the wall, Anna takes a pitchfork and drags decaying hay away from the wall to underneath the ladder. Professor Dugan tells her not to try pitching it outside. "I'll send one of the young men from the construction crew over."

Professor Dugan has already removed the dead snakes. She does not see signs of more snakes, although she cannot help feeling apprehensive. Standing near the wall, she peeps through a crack where cement is crumbling from between the rocks.

Bending low, she runs gloved hands along the wall. Near the bottom, a rock juts out from the rest. Underneath, she finds a hole almost large enough for her hand. Something touches her shoulder. Lunging forward, she struggles to keep from falling, too breathless to scream.

Jim grabs her arm. "Sorry, I didn't mean to scare you. Mr. Dugan told me to toss this hay outside."

She leans against the wall where she found the first crack. "There's the pitchfork."

"You're awfully pale. Maybe you should go outside and get some fresh air. It smells terrible in here. There's probably another dead snake in this hay. You'd think those federal men would have cleaned this out, but I guess they were only interested in Yankee bones."

She forces a grin. "I'll be all right in a minute. When you

touched my shoulder, I thought it was a snake."

He looks toward the ladder, steps closer and whispers. "I'm sorry for telling those guys where you were, but I didn't have a choice—they said they'd get Grandpa and Danny if I didn't help." He sighs and looks away.

"I got into this mess by accident. A boy who delivers for a grocery store asked me to finish making his deliveries because he was sick. He looked sick, so I said I would. Shortly after, he showed me a picture of a guy taking a package and handing me money. They said that if I didn't continue to work with them, I would wind up in jail for selling drugs or at the bottom of Beaver Lake, along with my brother and grandpa. I don't know how to get out without getting Grandpa and Danny hurt."

"I'll pray for you. I'm sure they plan to kill me." She clasps her hands and looks at the floor. "All I can do is pray, and I do that continually."

Jim kicks at a gravel. "Do you think that helps?"

"I'm sure of it. The Bible says, 'The fervent prayer of a righteous man avails much.' I'm not perfect, but I have faith, and I pray. Try it, Jim. Jesus will be with you if you ask."

"Maybe so, but my life's in a real mess." He sticks the pitchfork into the hay, tosses it outside as fast as he can, and returns to the work crew building the new barn.

Professor Dugan calls from the top of the ladder. "Anna, I'll pry these rotten boards loose if you'll come up and drag them into a pile. I'll have those guys haul them to the dump with the scraps from the new barn. At the end of the day, when everyone leaves, and I get those dead snakes buried, Mr. Tucker will spray this full of poison again."

"Is he able to do that, so soon after having heart surgery?"

"Jim will help him. I'd like to have a new floor put in next week while those guys are on the property."

Anna cannot believe what she is hearing. First, he lets Jim come inside, next a construction crew. They will find that tunnel for sure.

"Sir, can we put lots of insect granules inside and close the doors. Bart will put a floor in here when he comes home in the spring. He's good at building things. I'm afraid a construction crew will find the passage. With the new barn, we don't need this one."

"Maybe so. I'll think about it over the weekend."

When Carol goes to take her bath, Anna brings up the subject again. "Professor, I'm afraid for you to have a construction crew in the old barn. I found some cracks in the rock wall. I could look into that cell from one of them. I don't trust Jim. Others on the crew could be involved with dealing drugs or worse. If you wait on Bart, I know he'll put a floor in the barn for you."

Mary comes down the stairs and stands to listen. "Charles, I agree with Anna. I don't like the idea of anyone going in that old barn until the entire trial is over."

"I think you're both overreacting. No one can climb such a high rock wall as we have around the backyard, but I'll wait for Bart."

After Carol is asleep, Anna closes her door and removes her dad's guns from the top of her closet. Wiping them with a dry washcloth, she examines each one carefully before returning them to the closet and checking the shells. She takes her pistol from the holster and puts it on her nightstand with a clip beside it. She wants to be ready if Jim brings his friends around.

Anna is deep in a land of dreams when Carol shakes her bed and whispers. "Anna, something's making noise inside my wall."

"Don't turn the light on. Go get your daddy. Whisper." She puts a clip in her pistol, straps it on over her pajamas, and loads her dad's guns.

Carol and Professor Dugan appear at the door. In a low voice he says, "I called Miller. He's on the way."

"This is Jim's doing. I'm sure of it." She hands her boss one of her dad's guns. "It's loaded. Carol, get under my bed."

The panel slides to one side. Anna fires her gun, hits a figure on the shoulder, and hears someone tumbling down the stairs. He drops something that clunks all the way to the bottom. Dripping blood, a young man scrambles to get outside.

Professor Dugan yells, "Stop, or I'll shoot."

A teenage boy slumps to the floor, moaning.

Detectives arrive and cuff boys outside the rock fence, holding a ladder. Jim is one of them.

"Anna, you were right. Jim must have told the others about the passage. I'll get a deadbolt put on the outside door and hire a man with a backhoe to dig around the stable while snakes are in hibernation. I would destroy the old barn if it were not such a part of history. Too bad you don't have a snake detector."

Anna tilts her head to one side and grins. "Do you want one? I read an article in the paper about an old man looking for a home for his snake-hunting dog. The man is sick and having to move in with his daughter. She can't have dogs in her Boston apartment."

"Mary, what do you think about Carol having a dog?"

"I don't mind if it will live outside and not bark at the horse or us."

A big smile comes to his face. "Find the article and phone number. I'll call about it, first thing tomorrow morning."

Anna digs through the magazine rack until she finds the article saved from the paper. "Here it is."

While Anna clears away the breakfast dishes, Professor Dugan goes to call the man. He wears a big smile when he returns to the kitchen. "The old man and his daughter are coming over here this afternoon to make sure our yard is big enough for his dog, Curly, to have room to run and play. I figured the dog would be old, but he said Curly is a pup from a dog he owned for years. This one is almost two years old."

Mr. Mott and his daughter arrive at three thirty. Mr. Mott leads Curly through the house on a leash and releases him in the backyard. He is beautiful, colored like a collie, but Mr. Mott said he is a mixed breed. Instantly, Carol loves him. She tosses a rubber ball across the yard. "Fetch, Curly." In a flash, the dog gets the ball, returns it to Carol and plops down at her feet.

Mr. Mott laughs. "I named him Curly because he was always trying to curl up beside my feet so I could scratch his neck.

Anna brings Polka over, talking to both animals as she rubs and pats them. Polka leans her head low and whinnies. Curly whines, eases his nose close, and dances in front of the horse.

Mr. Mott leans on his cane, breathing hard. "This is an ideal place for Curly—a big yard, and a family to love him. I used to take Curly's mama around to different parks hunting poison snakes. He won't bother king snakes, but he hates rattlers, cottonmouth, and copperheads. There was a time when I could make good money catching and killing the poison ones. No more. The Game and Fish Commission doesn't want people killing rattlers."

"Mr. Mott, your article was interesting, but it didn't say if you are selling or giving away the dog to a good home. I need to know before we get too attached."

The old man rubs his chin. "Do you plan to keep him for a pet, or use him for hire?"

"I want a pet for my daughter. She's afraid of snakes. So am I. I don't want any part of catching them—only killing those in our yard."

He turns to Anna. "What about you, young lady?"

"I'm afraid of snakes, but I love animals. Curly will have a good home with us."

"You can have him at no charge. That is if I can visit, whenever I get back to town."

"You're welcome anytime. Tell me, though, if a snake comes into our yard, how do I get Curly to let us know? "

"Where is the last place you saw a snake?"

The professor points. "Under Carol's playhouse and in the barn."

The old man chuckles. "Come here, Curly. Come boy, sic 'em." He aims his cane underneath the playhouse.

The dog crawls partway underneath, sniffs the dirt, but soon returns wagging his tail.

"There are no snakes under there."

They go to the barn. Pointing to the ground in front of the door with his cane. Mr. Mott calls, "Sic-'em Curly."

Curly sniffs and runs around the building, barking, and scratching.

"Open the door and let him inside."

Professor Dugan points to Carol. "Anna, will you take her inside, to Mary."

When back at the barn, Anna sees the dog digging in one corner of the lower floor. "I thought this was solid concrete."

The old man holds tight to the door facing; his eyes follow the dog. "Not where he's digging. He's found something. My guess is a den. I'd pour a bottle of acid in that hole if I were you."

Professor Dugan steps away. "Mr. Mott, call your dog and put him on the leash. Anna, go call Mr. Tucker and get him to bring his poison, right now if he can."

Within twenty minutes, Mr. Tucker is pumping poison into the hole where Curly was digging. He covers the hole with a heavy piece of glass and shovels dirt around the edges. "That should do it. With the poison and icy weather blowing in, those snakes are not going to move. Dig them out tomorrow morning and chop their heads off."

"I have an important meeting tomorrow morning. Can it wait until late afternoon?"

"Sure, that's even better. They're not going anywhere."

Mr. Mott holds tight to Curly's leash. "I've got two more days until we leave for Boston; I want to keep Curly as long as I can."

"Certainly." Professor Dugan hands him a business card. "Call me and I'll pick him up when you're ready."

Monday morning, dressed for the cold weather, Anna and Carol take the metal detectors from the garage and go into the backyard. "Carol, let's check around the barn. I bet that's where the old captain would hide his treasure."

"Okay. I hope we find something besides old plows and nails."

Polka sticks her nose out of her new barn and whinnies.

Carol places her machine on the ground and runs to pet the horse. "Polka, if we find gold and jewels, I'll buy you something. Would you like a new saddle with gold and silver on the straps?"

Anna turns on her machine and runs it over the ground outside the barn. It makes the sound for metal detection. With her heel, she marks the dirt over the loudest spot before she continues around the old building. The same thing occurs at two more places. One is where Curly was digging for snakes.

Carol comes rushing over with her machine. "Wow! Maybe this is a big treasure. Do you want me to get the shovel?"

"I think we should wait until your daddy comes home. What if we dig up some big snakes? Even if we find a chest of gold coins, we'll need help."

"Okay, can I ride Polka?"

"I don't think I should lift a heavy saddle. Do you want to ride bareback, like an Indian princess?"

Excited, she nods. "I'll find some feathers to braid in my hair."

Both girls laugh. "Try riding first. Get on the top step of the playhouse. I'll bring Polka up beside it. You can take hold of her mane and pull yourself onto her back."

Carol frowns and shakes her head. "Won't that hurt her?"

"You're not heavy enough to hurt her. She'll barely know you've pulled on her mane."

She follows Anna's directions and is soon in the middle of Polka's back.

"Are you ready to guide her by yourself?"

"Yes, but will you stay close?"

Anna nods. "Okay, but don't kick her. I can't outrun a

horse." She lifts the reins to Carol. "Remember what you learned about right and left?"

"Yep, I salute with my right hand."

"Okay, when I say right, pull on the right side of the rein. If I say left, pull on the left side. Don't jerk or Polka will turn too fast. Pull gently so you don't hurt her mouth."

Carol nods. "I'm ready."

"Lightly touch your heels to her sides and say, 'Giddy-up, come on girl.'"

Polka moves forward.

"Right."

She turns to the right and moves around the yard. Before lunch, Carol can get on and off the horse by herself, make her start, stop, turn, and back up. She fills the watering tub and measures grain into the trough, exactly as told.

"Sister-friend, all you need is practice."

"Can I make her run?"

"No. Not until two weeks are up. You need lots of practice. When you are so good at walking her that you could sleep and not fall off, I'll let you run with her."

They go upstairs for a nap. "After we rest, we'll be ready to help your daddy dig out those snakes and maybe a treasure chest."

Anna is shocked from a sound sleep by someone banging on the front door. She peeps from behind the drapes of Carol's bedroom window, but shrubs hide the door. A brown UPS truck sits in the driveway. Gazing at the truck, she sees a teenage boy inside.

Carol is awake but does not make a sound. "Get in my closet." Carol does as told. Anna already has the pistol on her hip. The rifle is loaded when she hears glass breaking downstairs. She punches 911 on her cell phone. "Someone is breaking in." She tosses the open phone onto her bed and aims the rifle at the open bedroom door. The stairs creak louder than she has ever heard. Slowly, very slowly, someone advances. A hand holding a gun appears in front of the door. Anna slams the rifle barrel down on the hand. His gun roars and a bullet crashes into the wall; the intruder stumbles backward and falls into the stairwell, leaving his firearm at the top of the stairs.

Peeping around the door facing, she can see a young man dragging his companion across the carpet. Frightened eyes stare back at her. "Stop where you are unless you want a bullet." Sirens scream through the community and stop in the driveway, with blue lights flashing.

Detective Miller climbs through the broken window and unlocks the door. Carol does not come out of the closet until Anna calls to her. The little girl wraps her arms around Anna and holds on tight.

Detectives shake their heads. "If they keep coming, you'll get them all, one by one."

Carol runs to the refrigerator, takes out a bottle of cola, opens and pours it over a glass of ice. She pokes a straw into the bubbles, "This time I get two sips."

The teenage boys who broke into the Dugan home knocked a UPS driver unconscious and took his truck. The UPS employee has a concussion, but he should quickly recover. The boys will return to a juvenile facility—this is not their first offense.

Professor Dugan calls a contractor to have new front windows installed, and steel bars placed over all downstairs windows.

* * * * *

Bart opens another letter from Anna. She tells him about Carol, her friend Jackie, and her classes. Her letter describes a peaceful life.

He writes to Anna telling her about his classes, the cold weather, the food, and his friends. He does not tell her about the staph infection he got after stepping on a piece of glass or about falling into an icy river while building a bridge.

Chapter Fourteen

Detective Miller lays a hand on Anna's shoulder. "I usually encourage people to attend church, but you should pray at home for a while. Don't go to church, the library, or the mall. Don't leave the Dugan home for any reason and don't open the door to strangers.

Her mouth drops open. "I haven't bought Christmas presents."

"Order your gifts online."

"I can't; I don't have a credit card."

"If they enjoy books, go online and pick out titles. I'll go buy them for you."

It seems her only solution. The bookstore wraps them with beautiful paper and ribbons.

* * * * *

Professor Dugan with a shovel and Anna with a sharp hoe dig where Curly indicated there were snakes. He pulls out five small dead snakes and crushes more eggs. "Will we ever stop finding these things?"

"Sir, eggs that haven't hatched by now are probably no good, but I think we should dig all around the building and dig deep. My detector indicated metal in this location."

He leans on his shovel and grins. "Dig away while I dispose of these. Maybe you'll find a chest full of gold."

Anna's hoe clunks against something with a hollow sound. "I've found it." She squeals.

"Well, dig it up. You deserve to find something better than poison snakes."

Carol runs up and grabs a hoe. "I want to help. Remember, part of the gold is mine."

Professor Dugan touches her shoulder. "Hon, if you see a snake, alive or dead, run for the house."

She digs into the earth and yanks. With the last pull, a rusted plow point rolls out. "Oh—another old plow."

Anna continues to dig. "I'm not ready to give up."

Still leaning on his shovel, Professor Dugan holds a grin. "Don't overdo yourself; that doctor said for you to take it easy for six weeks."

The wide blade of her hoe pulls out more and more dirt. Breathless, she steps back and puts a hand on her side. "I'll try again after I rest a minute. The dirt is moist and soft; those snakes probably kept it stirred."

Carol jams her hoe into the hole—it clinks on metal. Giggling, she digs fast.

Professor Dugan chuckles. "Sis, maybe you can sell those plows for scrap metal and get enough for a candy bar."

"Don't laugh, Daddy." She tugs hard. "Help me, Anna. This one is big."

Anna digs on one side. The professor lifts several shovels of dirt from the hole. "She's right. This is big; it's a metal box of some kind."

All three of them dig, with dirt flying in all directions. The chest has an old-fashioned lock on one side. "Girls, I hate to break this lock. It may be worth more than what's inside."

"No, Daddy, if it didn't have treasure inside, it wouldn't be locked."

"You have a point. Besides, the metal is rusted and coming apart. I think there's a pair of bolt cutters in my dad's toolbox. I'll go look."

The girls continue to dig around the box until the sides are clear of dirt. Anna pushes the shovel underneath, pushes down on the handle, and pries the box upward. Carol starts to grab it.

"No, Carol! It could have snakes under it."

The little girl backs away, shaking her arms.

"Put your hoe under this side, and mine under the other. We'll pry it out of the hole."

The heavy box barely moves as the girls struggle. A slender snake, nearly two feet long, slips from among moldy, decaying boards underneath the chest. Whether from the cold or Mr. Tucker's poison, the reptile barely moves before Anna chops its head off.

Carol looks up at Anna with wide, frightened eyes. "It could have bit me."

"I'm glad it didn't. Stand back. That rotten board on top of the box may have been decoration over steel, but the metal under it may not be solid. Another snake might crawl out from that mushy rotten wood."

Professor Dugan returns with the cutters, clips and removes the lock. "Anna, be ready with your hoe when I raise this lid."

No snakes are in the box. The professor's mouth drops open at the sight of paper money from the 1800's—US currency—another stack contains Confederate dollars. "Anna, will you get some serving tongs from the kitchen, we don't want to touch this money with our bare hands. Who knows what kind of bacteria is on it."

"While you're in the house, call Mr. Tucker and ask him to

bring more poison. Tell him we found a live snake.

"Sir, is it all right if I ask him to come tomorrow? It's too cold for snakes to move about, and I would rather he didn't see our chest of money."

"That's a good idea."

Mary returns with Anna. She has two pairs of tongs and two plastic tubs. "We'll separate the money and wash it in bleach water."

The professor frowns. "I'm not sure about that; bleach could diminish the value."

"Daddy, is there enough money here to buy me a big house and a car?"

"I don't know, Carol. Are you planning to move away from me and your mama?"

"Someday, when I'm big, I'll move into my house, but I want to live close. The land behind this house has a 'For Sale' sign. Maybe, I can buy it and get a horse like Polka to eat the tall grass."

With tongs, Mary and Anna remove the mold-scented bills and place them in tubs. Underneath the bills, they find bars of gold.

"That's why the box is so heavy." Anna shrieks. "I knew it was more than paper. I'm going to dig at the other two places where the detector showed signs of metal."

Finally, the professor drags the box out of the hole. Underneath is a cluster of eggs and a passageway into a tangled maze. "Anna, are those snake tunnels?" Carol asks.

She nods. "I think so. Moles or gophers probably made the original burrows, but I'm sure snakes ate the animals years ago and took over their home. That's what snakes do. Come on.

Let's dig at the other locations."

Anna digs at one mark. Carol and Professor Dugan work the other. Mary takes the moldy paper inside and sprays it with disinfectant spray. Within an hour, they dig up two more chests with paper money and gold bars identical to the first, except no snakes or eggs.

They transfer the paper to a cardboard box, the bars to a plastic tub. Anna takes the box to the kitchen counter; Professor Dugan drags the tub into the sunroom. "Mary, should we call the FBI, or just take it to the bank?"

"I thought you told Carol and Anna they could have any treasure they find with the machines."

"We each get a third, but we can't turn two kids loose to go uptown with this much gold."

"Do you think it's worth close to a million?"

"I doubt that. Although, gold is at a high selling rate. Anna shouldn't have to worry about buying used books next semester."

"I think you should call the FBI and get an armed guard to escort you to the bank."

Anna and Carol with cola and lemonade sit silent. They look at each other with wide eyes, occasionally smiling. As anxiety builds, Carol giggles and they slap hands in a high five.

Mary turns to the girls. "Anna, what do you think we should do?"

"Call the FBI detectives and Detective Miller. Tell them we need to talk to them within an hour. And call the head person at your bank and ask him, or her, to meet here at the same time. I think it would be good for your lawyer to sit with us too. There may be regulations we are not aware of concerning old money. I would like to see it counted and stored in the vault, today. Plus, we need the Confederate money counted and placed in the vault or a safe deposit box. All of this is probably more valuable to collectors than in regular deposits."

Mary and the professor nod. "That sounds wise. Carol will list us as beneficiaries; who do you want to list?"

"You, Carol, and Bart are the only family I have. You are my parents now, and Carol and Bart are my sister and brother. I appreciate you keeping your promise to share with me. Like Carol, I want to buy some of that vacant land, and someday have a house built on it."

Mary gives Anna a hug. "Charles, you call the detectives—I'll call the banker and lawyer." She glances at the clock. "Hurry, dear. It's getting late."

Waiting for the detectives, banker, and lawyer, they eat ham sandwiches, chips, and cake. Carol can hardly sit still or be quiet long enough to chew her food. "Anna, if I have enough money, I want to buy the land behind this house. If you buy the land on the other side, we'll be neighbors."

Anna kisses her fingertips and touches them to Carol's cheek. "That sounds like a good idea, little sister. I don't want to live far away from you."

The banker arrives first, next the detectives, and the Dugans' lawyer. Professor Dugan explains the situation and his promise to the girls. He asks the banker if his bank can insure the treasure until the girls decide what they want to do with the money.

"Certainly, our bank is one of the largest in this area."

The lawyer lifts his hand. "Sir, one bank can't ensure the safety of such a large amount. In fact, it could exceed the limit of two institutions. Mr. and Mrs. Dugan and girls, you should consider dividing the assets between two or more banks, so your deposit does not exceed the insurable limit. Do you want me to call another banker to handle part of the investment?"

Anna nods.

Professor Dugan agrees. "Yes, please do."

The FBI men seem irritated at a request to participate in a banking transaction; still they agree to accompany the bankers and the treasure to the respective banks.

As soon as the second banker arrives and takes a seat, Anna raises her hand and stands. All conversation stops. "I want to insist that this entire transaction remain secret. I believe this family could be in grave danger if news of this leaks to the press."

The second banker winks at Anna and says, "Young lady, the gossip magazines will pay big for a story like this."

Anna clenches her teeth before speaking. "Sir, you will pay big if you or your bank leaks this story. My safety is at stake. So is your job. Guard this information as if members of your family were in danger from kidnappers."

His shoulders slump, his chin drops and he appears to sink lower into the couch cushions. "Oh, we won't tell. I know what you say is true."

After the visitors leave, Professor Dugan punches a number into the phone and clicks the speaker button. "Mr. Tucker, Anna was supposed to call you this afternoon. We found another live snake and a nest of eggs. I'm quite anxious to get rid of these critters before someone in my family dies. Is it too late for you to come back today? I'll pay you an extra fifty."

"Anna did call, but she said tomorrow. I need money, so for an extra fifty, I'll be there within twenty minutes."

Professor Dugan hangs up the phone and rushes toward the door. "Anna, Mary, bring some of those extra strong leaf bags. We need to get those treasure boxes out of sight. I'll store them in the garage tonight." He stops before going out the door. "Carol, if Danny comes with Mr. Tucker, don't mention the treasure chests or the money. He might tell his brother. Jim already wants to kill Anna. If he finds out about the treasure, his gang might come to kidnap one of you and blackmail us."

"I won't tell." She slides off her chair. "Mama, can we make chocolate chip cookies? Danny likes those best."

Mary smiles and reaches to hug her daughter. "To celebrate, we'll make a double batch, and Danny can take the extras home with him."

Danny sits in the truck as Mr. Tucker puts on his coveralls. Carol yells out the back door. "Come inside, Danny. Mama's making chocolate chip cookies. We can eat all we want."

He looks at his grandpa.

"That's fine, son. Run along, but mind your manners."

Danny nods and runs to follow Carol inside.

The kids sit in the sunroom with a platter of cookies and mugs of milk. Danny grins occasionally. Carol giggles continuously. "Danny, do you have a Christmas tree yet? Daddy said we may have to use our old fake tree."

"Grandpa said they're too expensive this year, and his chest hurts too much to cut one from the woods, besides we don't have money for presents. Grandma's funeral cost a lot."

Carol's smile fades, and she sits silently sipping her milk. Jumping from her chair, she runs to whisper in Mary's ear.

Mary pats her on the back. "Good idea."

"I'll be back in a minute, Danny. I have a surprise for you."

She brings the small battery operated tree from the center of the dining room table and sets it beside her friend. "This is for you. It's not big but it's pretty, and it plays a song. She pushes a button, and the tree plays *Oh Christmas Tree*. She goes away again and returns with three packages wrapped in red foil. "The big one is for you; the middle size is for Jim, and the small one is for your grandpa."

Danny runs his hand over the big package. "I don't have money to buy presents for you."

"Getting rid of the snakes is the best present we could have. When they are dead, I can ride Polka in the yard anytime. I've already learned how to get on and off, ride bareback, and how to make her turn. Maybe, when your grandpa gets better, and you don't have to stay and help him so much, you can come learn to ride, and play with my new dog. We're supposed to get him tomorrow."

Professor Dugan comes in the door. "Danny, your grandpa's ready to go."

"I'll have to make two or three trips to carry all these presents."

Anna dumps all the cookies into a zippered bag. "Carol, you can bring these and the small package. I'll take the other two, and Danny can carry the tree."

The old man leans on the truck. He looks tired but manages a smile. "Girls, thank you for everything. Money's awfully tight this year, but God always provides."

Anna puts the packages on the seat beside Danny, who carefully holds his tree. "Yes, he does. Thank you for coming over so late in the day to spray again. Surely, all those snakes will die this time."

"You dug up the den. I don't believe you'll find more, but they've been living here for years. If you see signs or dig up another den, give me a call."

"Yes, sir. Merry Christmas."

He tips his hat and gets in the truck.

Carol watches *'Rudolph'* on TV. Anna, Mary, and Professor Dugan read novels. Anna jumps when her phone rings. She stands, twirls around and almost falls over the coffee table. "Bart! Where are you? A call from Europe will cost a fortune. You're where? No kidding—in our driveway!" She runs to pull aside the drape. "It's Bart. He's here."

Professor Dugan grabs her arm. "Look through the magnifier and make sure before opening the door. Somebody could be playing a trick."

Feeling her eyes widen and her expression turn solemn, her voice quivers, "I will, sir."

She flips the porch light on and watches through the magnifier as he steps onto the porch. Flinging the door open, she squeals. "Bart, why didn't you tell me you were coming?"

He drops two duffels and folds her in his arms, their cheeks pressing together.

Lights, on the road, flicker in the distance. Grabbing the duffels, Professor Dugan steps back. "Come inside. You can carry on with that in the hall."

Anna introduces Bart to the Dugans before continuing her excited chatter. "How long do you get to stay?"

"I'm home, but I have to finish my military obligation in the Reserve while I go to school. Tomorrow, I need to go register for classes."

"I don't think you can. School is out for Christmas vacation, but I have a book listing all the classes. You can work out a schedule."

He sticks out his hand to Carol. "So this is the artist who sent me those pretty pictures."

"Bart, are you gonna stay with us?" Carol questions.

"After I visit a while, I'll call a taxi to take me to a hotel."

"You can sleep in my bed. I'll sleep in Anna's room. Is that okay, Mama?"

"You'll have to sleep on the folding cot. You wiggle too much to share Anna's bed."

"I can do that. Bart, will you stay?"

He looks at Mary and Professor Dugan.

The professor glances up from his book. "You'll have to work that out with the girls."

Mary smiles. "I'll show you where to put your things. I won't turn away Anna's friend."

Chapter Fifteen

Professor Dugan, on vacation until after Christmas, is still in his room when Anna goes down the stairs. At the kitchen counter, Mary holds a cup of coffee and a piece of toast. "Anna, I must go to work for a few hours. Do you mind cooking breakfast? I overslept."

Anna reaches for a skillet. "I'll hurry if you think you'll have time to eat bacon and eggs."

"I need to leave in a few minutes. I'm the designated person to open this morning."

"I should have come down earlier."

"This toast will hold me until the break." She waves a hand. "Charles put our old Christmas tree in the living room. If you want to set it up and decorate, I don't mind, but save the star and angel until we can all be together for Charles to read the Christmas story."

Anna moves close and whispers. "What do you think of Bart?"

"Handsome and well-mannered; I like him."

"He's the nicest guy I've ever known. He treats me like a princess."

Mary looks over her glasses and grins. "Then he's different from a brother. My brother called me rug rat and treated me like one until he graduated high school."

Anna smiles. "I'm glad to have Bart home. I say home because he says Fayetteville will be home until he graduates."

Mary lifts her purse and steps toward the door. "He's

welcome to stay here until school starts. I think you and Carol are safer while he's in the house."

"I'll tell him. That'll give him time to find something he can afford."

After breakfast, Bart sets the tree on its stand and helps string the lights.

"Anna, I need to drive down to see Aunt Alice."

"Maybe you can go on Sunday and attend church with her."

"Do you want to go?"

"I'll go another time. You should go by yourself and devote this time to her."

"I think you're right." He bites his lip, looks around, and lifts a box of ornaments.

Carol looks in the box. "We can put on everything except the angel and the star. Daddy reads the Bible while we hang those, and then we put presents under the tree and say a prayer to thank God for Jesus and all our blessings."

Bart straightens a string of lights. "I like your custom. When I get married, I want God as a major part of my family life. What do you think, Anna?"

"Yes, every day, then and now." She reaches for a sweater. "Let's go feed Polka an apple."

Carol runs to get her jacket. "Bart, I'll show you how I can ride bareback."

He grins and gives her a high-five. "Won't stingy Anna let you use her saddle?"

She giggles. "Anna's not stingy. The saddle's too heavy until her side gets well."

Panic showing on his face, he turns to Anna. "What's wrong with your side?"

"The doctor removed a cyst. I'm fine, except it hurts to lift something heavy."

"You never mentioned having a cyst."

"I didn't know until the night of the surgery, but everything is all right now." She slaps his back. "Let's go see Polka."

Carol runs ahead. Bart puts on his jacket and reaches for Anna's hand. "I want you to take care of yourself. I couldn't bear it if something happened to you. I was in anguish when I heard you married Jaeger, and you didn't answer my letters."

"I'm sorry. I was in a daze, and Jaeger must have destroyed your letters; I never got them." She looks away. "I guess it's a good thing that I can't remember much during that time with Jaeger. I believe he and his mama kept me drugged and set up the wedding. I certainly didn't love him." She clenches her teeth and shakes her head. "In fact, I despise him and his entire family."

She sighs and squeezes her arms tight against her chest. "Is it a sin to despise him? If it is, pray for me. I can't help how I feel. He's cruel. I was lucky to get away."

Gently, he pulls her into his arms. "Anna, don't think about Jaeger. I know those days were the worst of times for you, but I want to keep you safe and make you laugh again like you did when we were kids."

"That seems like ages ago."

"It does, but together we can bring back laughter."

Carol waves her hand and yells, "Anna, come on. I'm ready to ride. Bart, watch how I can get on." With her hands twisted in Polka's mane, Carol pulls herself onto the mare's back and touches the horse with her heels. "Giddy up, Polka."

"Way to go, girl," Bart shouts.

Carol rides Polka from one end of the yard to the other. Bart and Anna walk over to the old barn. "I told Professor Dugan that you are a good carpenter and will help put a floor in this barn when we get all the snakes killed."

"Snakes. What kind of snakes?"

She grins. "African black mambas."

He returns the grin. "Sure, and you plan to keep elephants in the stable."

"No; I'll use it for a garage." Looking up at him, she takes a deep breath. "We should find a seat. This story will take a while to explain."

A continuous frown covers his handsome face until she tells him every detail of the snake saga—except she does not mention the money and gold. "I thought my side was well, but digging with Carol made it hurt again. If not for that, I would be shoveling up every inch of ground around this building. I want to make sure no black mambas are living here when spring rolls around."

Bart takes the shovel standing against the barn. "This will give my arms a workout."

"Let's run the metal detectors around the barn a few times before you dig. We might find some Civil War Uniform buttons. The Army Department took the one's Carol and I found."

"The Army?" He looks puzzled.

Anna blinks. "That's another long story. I'll tell you all about that when we go inside to warm up."

Before going inside the barn to get the detectors, he grins and nods. "This should be fun. I remember when your dad bought those machines. I wanted one of my own, but I knew Aunt Alice couldn't afford such an expensive toy."

"Professor Dugan is supposed to get Carol's dog from the veterinarian's this afternoon. Curly hates snakes. He found the location of a big den. I like having him close when I'm digging."

"Maybe we'll find treasure instead of snakes. Civil War relics are valuable—guns, sabers, and even musket balls. That old sea captain might have saved pearls or diamonds from his voyages into Africa." He pauses to grin at Anna. "Surely, he brought home something more valuable than snakes."

Two hours pass while Bart runs the detector around and inside the barn. He finds one rusty metal button, two square nails, and a short chain. In one corner of the basement, the machine clicks loudly. A large flat rock fits snug within a two-foot square. Bart grabs the shovel. "This is it." Grinning, he pries out the rock and digs fast and steady.

Anna sees no signs of snake tunnels. With a scraping noise, the shovel strikes metal.

"I've found it." With the shovel point, he pries, but it will not budge. "It may be a lid to a treasure box or chest."

"I found a pair of ice tongs hanging in what I'm guessing was a tack room. Do you think you could pull it out with tongs?"

"I bet that'll work. Will you get them while I dig a little more?"

"Sure." Anna returns dragging the tongs and a pry bar. "I'm so eager to see what's inside there. I'm tempted to reach in with my hands, but people rarely survive a black mamba's bite."

He wipes the back of his hand across his forehead. "Is the hoe where you can grab it?"

Glancing at the hoe standing against the inside wall, Anna nods. "Within arm's reach."

He winks. "If I can budge it with these tongs, jam the pry bar underneath."

Groaning, he pulls. The box slides about an inch. Twisting the tongs, Bart raises the box one inch at a time until Anna can get the bar under the edge. "It must be full of rocks."

"Diamonds and rubies." She giggles. "Or maybe gold."

"Anna," Carol calls from the barn door.

"We're in the basement. Be careful, if you get on the ladder. I can't help you now."

"I'll watch from here. It looks dark down there."

Bart drops the tongs and sticks the shovel under the box. Anna takes a deep breath. "Carol, will you run in the house and get a flashlight from the kitchen drawer?"

The little girl disappears.

The heavy box is stuck. Exhausted, Bart and Anna release the shovel and pry bar, leaving the box to rest on them. They lean against the wall and smile when they hear Curly bark and Professor Dugan call to Carol.

Helped by her daddy, Carol descends the ladder and holds the flashlight while the two men pull the box from the hole and break open the lid. Whining, Curly stands at the door. Spear points and two rough handled hatchets are at the top of the chest. Further down they find a leather pouch containing shark teeth; another holds pearls. Several slabs of ivory come out next. On the bottom, they find four gold bars.

Carol squeals. "Remember, Daddy, part is mine."

"Bart and I helped. We deserve a share. Don't you think we should divided it equally?"

"I guess so." She frowns, and then a little smile forms. "At least they didn't dig up more snakes."

Professor Dugan lifts Curly and sets him on the basement floor. The dog whimpers and runs from corner to corner, but does not bark until Anna swings open the fake wall that serves as a door to the tunnel. He runs inside, stopping at a crack in the wall between the stable and tunnel. He barks and scratches at the crumbling concrete.

"Oh, no." Anna moans. "Not more snakes."

Professor Dugan grabs a pickaxe balanced over two large spikes in the old barn. "Better to find out now than later." He brings the point down hard near the cracked concrete.

Bart reaches for the pick, swings it several times, breaking loose numerous large chunks. Anna rakes away smaller pieces with the hoe. Professor Dugan flips over the largest section with his shovel. From the barn floor, a hard packed burrow runs under the rock hallway.

Professor Dugan steps away, shaking his head. "We may have to sell everything in the treasure chest to pay for getting rid of these snakes. If they've tunneled into the front yard, we'll have to alert the Environmental Protection Agency. The entire community could be in danger."

Carol whines, "Not my share."

"Maybe everyone's share. We might even have to tear the house down if they're under the foundation."

"Daddy, not my room."

"Especially your room, it's on this side of the house."

She runs to the ladder, climbs up and runs outside. Curly follows her to the ladder, whines once, and runs back to where Bart is breaking more concrete.

The burrow ends at the outer edge of the hall. A slender snake coils there. It tries to lift its head but is apparently sick from Mr. Tucker's poison. It makes a strange sound and tightens its loop. Bart grabs the hoe from Anna. With one hard chop, the snake is dead.

Professor Dugan grabs Curly and sets him in the barn, above the ladder. "We don't need that dog tearing a snake apart and slinging blood on us."

"Sir, I think this is the end of the burrow. I'll haul this serpent outside and then we can look more." After burying the dead snake, Bart tears out the nest and brings Curly back to explore. He does not indicate that more snakes are in or around the barn and hallway.

Anna prepares lunch while Professor Dugan and Bart bring the treasure into the sunroom.

Mary comes home in time to eat with the family. She calls another banker suggested by the lawyer. He arrives at two, accompanied by a security guard. They count all the items and name them on duplicate records, before the banker and his guard haul them away to the vault. They list Bart as owning twenty-five percent of the treasure.

"Professor, do you have a wheelbarrow?"

He nods. "In the garage. I use it to haul mulch to the flowers and trees in the front yard."

"If you'll buy three or four bags of cement mix, I'll mix it in the wheelbarrow and patch those holes we dug in the barn—before something else burrows in there. If it were mine, I'd toss in a few handfuls of bug granules and sulfur before the cement. Also, you might want to have enough lumber delivered to put in a new floor where Danny broke through those rotten boards. I can work on replacing the floor next week, and have it finished before school starts in January."

"Good idea. I'll try to get it delivered tomorrow. What do you think I should order—about thirty oak, two-by-six boards?"

"If you don't have to work tomorrow, why don't we drive out to St. Paul? I went there once with a friend of mine. His relatives owned a sawmill and sold lumber cut to customer specifications. Thick, rough oak is what I suggest, and we'll need a good screw gun and long screws. It takes a powerful man to drive nails into thick oak lumber, and nails tend to work out as the lumber dries. Anna, did Jaeger take your dad's carpenter tools?"

Hearing her name, she turns. "What do you need?"

"A screw gun, to use in flooring the barn."

"Dad's gun is in storage at Russellville, but it will cost half as much in gas to go after it as a new one will cost. Professor, when we get a new floor in the barn, and you have a place to store them, you can bring all those tools up here."

He takes a sip of coffee. "I probably wouldn't know how to use most of them, but they will be handy for Bart."

Grinning, Bart rubs his hands together. "I'm eager to begin. I love building. Someday, I hope to build my home, although that's a long way off. I worked on a construction crew in the Marines—mostly bridges and temporary buildings. I want to get a civil engineering degree."

Turning to face him, Anna leans against the cabinet. "Bart, be careful as you go around this town. Jaeger's in jail, but he has friends definitely as evil. He was extremely jealous of you and said he hoped you didn't make it home."

"Jaeger and his friends are cowards. They pick on girls and guys much smaller."

"That's just it. They're cowards that will shoot you in the

back or cut the brake lines on your truck."

"I'll be careful."

Mary brings an armload of folders from her car. "Anna, do you mind cooking supper? Since I left work early, I brought these papers to complete at home."

"I love to cook. Should I fry the chicken that's in the meat tray?"

Mary smiles. "Again, Carol requested fried chicken and mashed potatoes."

Glancing at Carol, they give each other okay signs. "Fried chicken is on the menu."

Before taking the chicken from the refrigerator, Anna turns on the oven, takes a frozen pie crust from the freezer, and mixes the ingredients for a pie. She has never made a coconut pie for the Dugans but remembers that it is Bart's favorite.

Carol sets the plates and silverware on the table, fills the glasses with ice and drops a napkin beside each plate. "Since we have fried chicken, I got the big dinner napkins. Bart, they're strong enough to last through the peach pie."

Picking her up, he tosses her into the air and catches her. "I don't think we have peach pie."

She nods. "I bet we do. Anna always makes peach pie when she fries chicken. It's the one I like best, except for chocolate cake."

He winks at her. "Peach pie and chocolate cake are very special. I have many favorites. You and Anna are my favorite girls."

Shaking her head, she demands, "Put me down, I can't be your girl. Danny's my boyfriend."

"Okay, I wouldn't want Danny gunning for me. Besides

Anna's mighty pretty."

Turning to take biscuits from the oven, Anna pretends not to hear. "Will you set the butter and honey on the table?"

After the meal, Anna gets up to clear the table. "Mary, should we have pie now or later?"

"Carol needs to get her bath and go to bed. She yawned through supper."

"I'll serve it now." She cuts the coconut pie and slides it onto dessert plates, although it is not cool enough to stand firm.

Carol bends close looking at the pie and whispers to Bart, "I never ate this kind of pie. It's got fuzzy stuff in it."

"It's coconut. All little monkeys like coconut."

She slugs him on the arm. "I'm not a monkey."

"Take a bite. It's another one of my favorites."

She lifts a bite to her mouth and moves it around with her tongue. "It tastes good, but those fuzzy things will take a while to chew."

After dessert, Mary goes to the den with her paperwork. Bart sits explaining to Professor Dugan what he thinks they need to do about putting a floor in the barn. Carol trudges upstairs to take her bath; Anna follows and is soon pulling a blanket around her shoulders, remembering Bart's gentle hug as he wrapped his arms around her. She is deep in dreams when he comes up the stairs.

Chapter Sixteen

Bart holds Anna as she kicks and gasps for breath. "Let me go, Jaeger! Let me go."

"Wake up, Anna. Wake up." He washes her face with a cold cloth.

Opening her eyes, she relaxes against his chest. "I was having a nightmare."

"A terrible nightmare. Carol brought you a cup of water. Sit up and take a drink?"

Her hand trembles as she takes the small plastic container. "Thank you. Every night I make myself think happy thoughts before I go to sleep. Still, sometimes I wake up dreaming Jaeger's choking me until I can't breathe."

"He choked you?"

Anna nods. "Until I passed out. The smallest disagreement turned him into a raving madman, but he was sane enough not to hit me and make bruises where others could see—until the night before I escaped. The police have a picture of that bruise."

Carol kneels beside Anna, tears on her cheeks. Mary stands in the doorway. "You need to see one of the counselors at my office. These nightmares have continued too long. You may need serious treatment before you can overcome Jaeger's cruelty."

"I'm fine during the day, but I can't keep him from returning as a bad dream. If it continues after the trial is over, I'll make an appointment with a counselor."

Mary takes Carol's hand. "Let's go downstairs and warm

some milk. Bart, you and Anna, come along in a few minutes. We'll have milk and graham crackers."

Anna wakes early the next morning and is cooking breakfast when Mary comes down the stairs. "I thought you might sleep later after such a restless night."

"I'm sorry that I woke you again. I'd stop it if I knew how."

"I understand. Maybe you ought to take an afternoon nap with Carol. I think you're trying to do too much, too soon after surgery."

"I may take a nap today. Now that the snakes seem to be gone, I'll rest better. Curly didn't show signs of agitation after the last one disappeared. He's a good dog. I'm glad he made instant friends with Carol and Polka."

"So am I. Yesterday was a very eventful day. I shouldn't have to bring work home tonight, so we'll put the star and angel on the tree after supper."

"Do you want me to fix the prime rib roast for the celebration?"

"That will be wonderful." She hugs Anna.

Bart comes down the stairs in jeans and a long-sleeved tee shirt. Giggling and still in her pajamas, Carol holds his hand.

"What's for breakfast? It smells delicious."

"Sausage, scrambled eggs, and cinnamon rolls."

He licks his lips and rubs his stomach. "Carol said she'll help put a floor in the barn if we get boards today. She'll need a good meal if she's going to maneuver a hammer."

She giggles and swings on his arm. "I didn't say that. I'll watch and put bandages on your mashed fingers."

"Bart, please take those rolls from the oven and put them on the sunroom table. Carol, will you wash your hands and set the table. We're almost ready to eat." She places eggs on a platter. "Mary, go ahead and fill your plate. I know you have to hurry."

Mary takes Carol's hand. "Let's hold hands. Bart, will you say grace. It may be a while before Charles is ready."

Bart takes one of Anna's hands; Mary holds the other. With his large muscular fingers wrapped around hers, Anna finds it hard to concentrate past his first sentence: "Lord, keep us all safe on this busy day, and . . . ."

"Amen." Professor Dugans voice echoes after Bart's closing. "It's a beautiful day to work outside. I'm excited about replacing that rotten floor in the barn, but Anna, I hate to leave you and Carol here by yourselves while we're gone to get lumber. I worry that some of Jaeger's gang might come around."

"We'll be fine. Most of the morning, we'll spend preparing for tonight's dinner. You'll probably be home before we venture outside."

Carol frowns. "I want to ride Polka and play with Curly."

Anna bends to whisper in her ear.

The little girl grins. "Okay."

Mary eats quickly and leaves. Professor Dugan and Bart are not far behind her.

"Carol, in the bottom drawer of my dresser is a box of cookie cutters. If you will run up and get them, I'll start mixing the dough."

"Okay."

It is not long until the cutters stretch across the counter. "The horses are pretty. Can we make them with Polka spots?"

"Sure. I used these when I was a little girl. Did you find a dog shape? My pup's name was Rascal. He looked a lot like Curly."

"What happened to Rascal?"

"He disappeared. Dad thought Jaeger shot him because Rascal went into their field. Hey, let's not talk about sad things. Making cookies is a happy time."

"Okay; what about frosting? How do we make the colors?"

"Your mama has food coloring; we'll mix until we have the colors we want."

When the clock strikes eleven, six dozen decorated cookies wait for frosting to dry.

"Carol, after lunch, we'll wrap them in plastic wrap with ribbons ties. Tonight we'll tie them on the tree."

Carol sighs and removes her frosting smeared apron. "They're pretty, but I'm tired of cookies. I want to ride Polka."

"You're good at riding bareback. Do you want to try the saddle this afternoon? Bart can lift it onto Polka."

She nods vigorously. "Can I make her trot?"

"Not yet. You need to learn a few more things."

The gate slides open. Professor Dugan's truck drives through the opening pulling a rented trailer with a heavy load of lumber.

"Carol, fill two big glasses with ice while I make them some sandwiches. They'll be thirsty. It's warm today."

Professor Dugan and Bart gulp lemonade and wolf the sandwiches in a rush to start work on the barn.

"Bart, Anna said I can use the saddle if you put it on Polka."

He picks her up and tosses her into the air. "It'll cost a white horse with chocolate spots. I have my eye on one with a pecan saddle."

"I made that one for you, the chocolate one for Daddy, and the Christmas tree with silver balls for Mom."

Carol goes with Bart to put the saddle on the horse while

Anna sets out rolls to rise, and peels potatoes, leaving them in a pan of cold water until time to finish cooking supper. She takes off her apron and goes outside in time to see Carol trying to dismount while Polka is walking.

"Whoa! Polka, Whoa! Anna runs to help Carol. "What were you trying to do?"

"Stand in the stirrup, but I slipped."

Anna frowns. "I told you no tricks. If you want to ride my horse, you have to follow my teaching. Go wash your skinned arm and I'll put medicine on it."

"Anna, are you still mad at me?"

"Sister-friend, I was upset that you fell."

"But, you told me no tricks until you said I could do one."

"Disobeying caused you a skinned arm and prevented you from riding more today."

"I didn't hurt Polka."

"No, you hurt yourself. I'm responsible for you. If you disregard what I tell you, your parents will not trust me as a nanny and want to hire an older woman with more experience."

"I'm sorry, Anna. I won't try any more tricks, and I'll mind what you tell me."

"Okay, we'll forget about this as long as it doesn't happen again. Rest until dinner's ready." She grins and lowers her voice to a whisper. "We'll be sister friends unless you try to steal Bart away from me. I changed my mind—he is my boyfriend, but it's our secret, okay."

Carol giggles. "A sister secret?"

Anna gives her a thumbs up and winks. "A sister secret."

The roast is fork tender. Bart cannot say enough about the meal. "Military food is okay, but nothing was this good."

"How is the barn floor coming along?" Mary asks.

"Slower than I hoped. We bought bridge timber, so we can drive a car or truck into the barn and never worry about falling through. The man at the mill said that unless termites get to it, oak bridge timber should last more than a hundred years when under a good roof."

Mary lifts her eyebrows. "I doubt any of us will need it to last longer."

Professor Dugan reads from the Bible about the birth of Jesus while Anna and Bart hang cookies and tiny angels on the tree. Curled on the couch with her head in Mary's lap, Carol watches and offers advice, but when it is time to hang the star and the big angel, Bart lifts her high so she can place them on the tallest part of the tree.

While the Dugans nibble decorated cookies, Bart asks Anna if she wants to see the new barn floor. "Yes, I wanted to go out there earlier, but I was afraid dinner might burn while I was gone. I'll get a couple of flashlights. I know it's too cold for snakes, and mambas don't come out at night. Still I would die of fright if I stepped on anything resembling a snake."

A full moon lights the sky almost as bright as day. Polka neighs and follows them to the barn door. Only four boards are in place, but enough that Anna knows it will be strong and safe.

Standing at the door, Bart reaches for her hand. "Anna, I know we have years of school ahead of us, but I want you to know that I love you. I've always loved you, and I want you for my wife as soon as I can support you. Will you wear my engagement ring? I don't want anyone thinking you are unattached."

"This is a surprise." She stammers, "I didn't know you felt

this way. I—I'm afraid I can't be a good wife to you or anyone. Jaeger was so cruel that, I just don't know. I panic when anyone hugs me tight." Leaning her head against his chest, she sobs, dampening his shirt with tears.

"Don't cry, Anna. Don't cry. You don't have to answer tonight. Only remember that I love you, and I'll never be cruel and treat you with disrespect."

"I know that. Things have been crazy this year. Mary thinks I need to see a therapist." She rubs her eyes with her fingertips. "Are you willing to wait for me to work this out?"

"I'll wait as long as it takes. I want us to have love and marriage like your mom and dad, and like the Dugans seem to have."

She sniffs. "Maybe, with help, I can get over Jaeger's cruelty. You can give me a ring, or we can simply make promises to each other. Following the trial, I'll see a therapist. After a while, maybe I'll be the kind of girl you need."

He pulls her close—closer until their lips touch soft and gentle. She trembles, but does not pull away.

Chapter Seventeen

Anna is up early to bake a breakfast casserole and refrigerator rolls. Bart comes into the kitchen with a pad of graph paper in his hand. Tossing the paper onto the table, he whispers, "Can I get a kiss while we're alone?"

She lifts her mouth to kiss his cheek, but he moves, and their lips touch. He holds her face gently with both hands. "Remember, I love you, Anna."

A pan of hot bread clatters to the top of the stove. "That potholder is too thin." She shakes her hand and sticks it under cold running water.

"Is your hand blistered?"

"No, but it got a little too warm."

"Mama, Daddy, Anna, it's Christmas morning. Can we open presents now?" In pajamas and bathrobes, the family comes down the stairs holding hands. Within minutes, Christmas wrap and presents cover the living room floor.

Bart sits beside Anna on the loveseat. The room is suddenly quiet as he holds out a small package. "This is not a Christmas present, and if you're not ready to make a commitment, store it away until you want to wear it."

Reaching, her right-hand trembles. She pulls it away and holds out her left hand.

He drops onto one knee, flips open a white leather box lined with red velvet and takes out a gold ring with a circle of tiny diamonds around a ruby. "Anna, will you marry me when you feel the time is right?"

"I will—when the time is right." Tears fill her eyes, although her face smiles.

His lips lean toward hers, but Carol pushes in front of him. "Let me see your ring. I like the red diamond."

Still holding Anna's hand, Bart whispers, "This is an engagement ring—until I can afford better."

Anna stands, holding up her left hand. "Breakfast is getting cold. On this beautiful Christmas morning, is it all right if we eat in the sunroom? In there, I can watch sun-sparkles dance on my ring."

Bart lifts the casserole, Mary takes glasses, Professor Dugan carries the coffee pot, and Carol skips in with napkins across her arm. Anna empties warm rolls onto a tray. Butter and strawberry jelly are on the table along with silverware and Christmas plates. Single file, they advance with their contributions. Bart, with a bass voice, sings, "Go tell it on the mountain, over the hills and everywhere. Go tell it on the mountain that Jesus Christ is born."

Mary joins him, but Anna stands smiling. "Bart, I didn't know you could sing like that."

He laughs. "I've never been this happy before."

Kissing her fingertips, Anna touches them to his cheek.

Carol, one knee on her chair, stretches her neck toward a soup tureen. "Anna, what's in the big bowl?"

"Chocolate gravy. It was a tradition in my family. Mom always made it on Christmas morning. We spooned it over buttered rolls. It's not too sweet if you eat your casserole first."

Mary smiles and looks at Carol. "I guess it's all right one day out of the year. Charles, will you offer thanks for our blessings?" Everyone holds hands and bows.

As soon as her dad says, Amen, Carol is reaching for rolls and chocolate gravy.

Mary takes the spoon. "Hon, you have to eat a serving of casserole first."

Frowning, the little girl takes a bite. "It's not bad; it tastes like sausage."

Mary smiles. "Anna makes it with sausage and eggs, and it's very good."

Carol eats fast, chewing little until her casserole is gone. "Mom, can I save my chocolate until later? I want to try my new saddle on Polka."

"Your saddle is not as heavy as Anna's, but it's too heavy for you to lift. Someone must help, and we're still eating. You have to wait until everyone is finished."

With a scowl, she takes a bite of the chocolate Anna dipped into a small bowl. "How come it takes grown-ups so long to eat?"

Bart reaches for the pad of graph paper and lays it on the table. "Professor Dugan, when you finish eating, I have something for you to consider. I drew a sketch of the basement, showing how I could make it into an apartment—that is if you'll rent it to me. As soon as I finish the barn floor, I could install a small bath and kitchen, and put up walls for bedrooms. Anna could store her things in one room and stop paying rent on storage in Russellville." He shifts in his chair and haltingly continues.

"A basement is warmer in winter and cooler in summer than above ground rooms, so a small Amish heater and a fan will be all I'll need for heating and cooling. I can do all the work myself. I'm a good cook, and I'm willing to do yard work and help out around the place to help reduce the rent."

Professor Dugan takes a sip of coffee and looks at Mary. "We'll talk it over and let you know tomorrow. We don't want to jump into anything that will disturb our family life. If we do agree, we will expect you to eat and stay in your apartment most of the time unless you have an invitation." He clears his throat and pauses to look around the table.

"We're not selfish, merely quiet people. We read and watch educational programs in the evenings. Anna and Carol spend a lot of fun time together. I think you can understand our not wanting to disrupt that relationship."

"Mama, may I be excused?"

Mary nods. Carol puts on her jacket and goes outside with an apple for Polka.

Professor Dugan continues, "Last winter, we almost lost our little girl to sickness. We hired Anna to keep her at home, so she can stay inside during bad weather. She has adopted Anna as a sister and friend. We no longer have discipline problems with Carol, and we believe she is learning more than she would with a licensed tutor."

Mary puts her napkin on her plate and pushes back her chair. "What Charles says is very important to Carol, but we love Anna too. She's part of our family. If you and Anna get married, you will be family as well, but now I feel it's important for her to have private time—time to work out problems of the last year."

Anna picks up the leftover casserole and takes it to the kitchen; still she can plainly hear the conversation in the sunroom.

"We are not using the basement and would be happy for you to use it, but we don't want to force Anna into giving up time that she needs to work through difficulties. Working with counselors has given me the opportunity to observe abused individuals. Jaeger was an abuser, and she needs time before she can run to you with open arms and engage in a healthy relationship. That's why Charles says we would expect you to eat and stay in your apartment most of the time unless you have an invitation to join us."

"I understand those issues. I sense Anna pulling away when I try to hug her. I know it's because of Jaeger. I love her and want to hold her close, but I'm willing to give her as much space and time as she needs."

Bart fumbles with the tablet of graph paper. "I plan to sign up for eighteen class credits. When school starts, I'll need to spend my spare time studying. You'll see very little of me. Tomorrow will be soon enough to let me know about the basement. I'll have a week to find an apartment. Now, if you'll excuse me, I'll take Carol's saddle out and help her put it on Polka."

Bart leaves for the backyard; Professor Dugan goes upstairs, and Mary brings the chocolate gravy to the kitchen cabinet. "Thank you, Mary. I love Bart, but I do need space for a while."

"I forgot to tell you that Charles called a carpenter to put in a solid wall with a dead-bolt door separating the stairwell going down to the basement."

"Good, I would trust Bart with my life, but Carol and I need privacy."

* * * * *

Bart and Anna make schedules for the new semester and are

at the front of the line on the first day of registration. Anna follows the advice of Professor Dugan and does not take night classes. She takes enough hours to meet scholarship requirements but cannot take as many as she wants, because she must be home to care for Carol in the afternoon.

With Professor Dugans consent, Bart adds a bathroom and small kitchen to the large basement and puts up dividing walls to separate three corners into bedrooms. Carol and Anna help with holding boards and measuring.

Bart has a three-bedroom apartment by the middle of January. He enters his new home from the old garage tunnel. Bart and the professor make a trip to Russellville, rent a truck and bring back Anna's stored belongings. He will use most of the furniture and household goods. One bedroom holds Anna's extra clothes, personal things, and collectibles.

He installs an automatic garage door to the old stable. It has enough room for his small truck and Anna's car; they refer to it as Bart's garage. He takes Anna to and from school, leaving her car inside.

Jackie and Anna do not have the same class schedule and rarely see each other. Occasionally, they meet in a hallway and exchange high fives. Jackie's new boyfriend drives her to and from school.

When Bart moved into his apartment, Carol moved back into her room. She is proud of the new wall and door with a deadbolt. Her daddy gives firm instructions, "Never open that door except in an emergency." Bart's apartment also has a new door with a deadbolt. When he comes to visit, he enters through the kitchen or the front door.

As the court date draws near, Anna becomes more nervous.

The backfire of a car or any loud noise makes her jump. She wears the pistol on her hip when she and Carol are alone in the house, and keeps the drapes closed.

Anna watches the news on her computer after Carol is in bed. About to fall asleep while reading an assignment, she glances up in time to see the latest report. Unknown gunmen overtook guards, killing Jaeger, his dad, and two boys from the gang as they were leaving the courthouse on their way to the county jail. Anna speculates that drug dealers were afraid the men and boys would plea bargain with information about the drug cartel.

Her mind in a whirl, she wants to talk to someone. She reasons that Mary and Professor Dugan are asleep; Bart is studying for a big test—she does not want to distract him; most likely, Jackie is asleep, and little Carol would not understand. She tries again to read the assignment but cannot concentrate.

Remembering words from her mom—"When you can't sleep, read the Bible and God will give you rest."—Anna takes her Bible from the bookshelf. A marker is at I Samuel. Anna begins to read, sympathizing with David as King Saul pursues him. When her eyelids get heavy, she returns the Bible to the shelf, pulls her blanket up, prays for her new family, for Jim and his family, and falls asleep still praying.

Anna is cooking breakfast when Detective Miller calls. "Did you listen to the news last night or this morning?"

"I saw it on my computer. Does that eliminate the trial? Am I still in danger?"

"I think they'll leave you alone since Jaeger, his dad, and Jim Tucker were the only ones you knew anything about."

She takes a deep breath. "I didn't hear Jim's name on the

news, but I wondered about him. I sympathize with his grandpa and little brother."

"Yeah, but that's what happens when someone deals with the Devil."

"Are you positive Jaeger was killed and not one of the guys coming to kill him?"

"Jaeger died from a knife injury. I didn't see the body, but I'm sure attendants wouldn't make a mistake like that. Let it go, Anna. I know Jaeger was cruel, and you've been worried for a long time, but he can't come back from Hades to hurt you."

She pauses, questions whirling in her head. "I hear you, but I know that Jaeger had never been to a dentist or a hospital, so he wouldn't have dental records or X-rays for the authorities to check."

"Let it go. It was Jaeger."

"Well, what should I do now? Will I get a letter from the court saying I don't have to show up?"

"You'll get a phone call or paper notice, but don't worry about it. You don't have to do anything."

She gets a glass of ice from the icemaker, pours cola over it and sits at the bar sipping through a straw. Carol will be disappointed that she was not awake to get her sip.

* * * * *

While getting ready for class, Bart listens to the news on his computer. Hearing about Jaeger, Bart's first reaction is to shout, "Yeah!" Feeling guilty about his joy, he drops to his knees. "Lord, I am thankful for all my blessings and your wisdom."

Chapter Eighteen

For days, television reporters rehash questions—"Why were the prisoners not shackled and flanked by more armed guards?" Public opinion seems to be that the death of kidnappers and drug dealers is a good thing. Therefore, reporters drop the story to discuss the weather.

January is cold, with rain, and light snow. Afternoons, Carol and Anna stay inside reading books, playing games, cooking and wishing they could ride. Polka and Curly stay in the new barn making use of the hay Professor Dugan bought.

Now that Anna is not afraid to drive her car to school, Bart leaves early to meet with partners on projects for his engineering classes. He returns after supper when Carol is in bed. Anna watches his truck pull through the gate and roll into his garage. She waves from her window but, in the dark, cannot see if he returns the wave.

After a few sessions with a counselor, Anna begins to understand her fears. During the day, she still jumps at shadows and wears her gun when possible. Thankfully, she rarely has nightmares of Jaeger's brutality and often dreams of Bart's gentle kiss and tender embrace.

Bart has a fixed invitation for dinner on Friday night. Mary and Professor Dugan usually visit with friends. Carol hangs onto Bart, arguing that she does not need to go to bed before nine.

"Anna, can we move the sunroom table to one end of the room so that we can dance?" Bart asks. "I noticed the old record player and dance records when we moved your things."

"That sounds like fun. I haven't danced for almost a year. Help me scoot the table against the wall. I'll move the chairs while you get records and the player."

While he is gone, Anna puts Carol to bed, changes into tights, soft shoes, and a full skirt. They start with a waltz. Bart and Anna are doing the jitterbug when Mary and the professor return. Smiling, they watch for a moment before going upstairs. At the end of the song, Anna pulls Bart into her arms and kisses him on the lips. "I forgot how much fun it is to dance with you."

"I didn't forget." He returns the kiss and holds her gently.

"Professor Dugan gave me two tickets to the Valentine Dance at the Country Club. He and Mary aren't going. Will you go with me?"

Clasping her hands, she giggles. "I'd love to. I've heard the Country Club has a nice dance floor, and their band plays the old songs—perfect for us—we learned on those."

* * * * *

Saturday morning, Anna goes to the mall looking for a dress. She finds the perfect jade green, with a full flowing skirt, but the price is more than she has ever paid for a dress. She returns it to the rack and tells the sales girl, "It fits my body, but not my budget."

She leaves that store and goes to a consignment shop. She finds a black dress with a full skirt of soft material; it has a red satin cummerbund with long streamers from a bow at the back. She likes it as much as the first; it looks new, and the price is less than half of the green. She leaves the store humming, with the dress in a bag.

"What shoes will you wear?" Mary asks.

"I have a pair of black dancing shoes with suede soles; they're comfortable."

"What will Bart wear?"

"I don't know. Do you think it will offend him if I ask?"

"It might, but he needs to wear a black tuxedo and red bow tie. Do you want me to ask and offer to help find something affordable?"

"If you don't mind? Mr. Prince paid me for one of my horses; I spent part of it, but I can give you two hundred toward a tuxedo, a new shirt, and bowtie." She shrugs and grins. "I guess I could take money out of the savings account from the treasure chests, but if I don't have to use that, I want to keep it for land and a house."

"It's yours to do with as you wish."

"Bart doesn't have to know the full price of everything. I enjoy finding bargains—to me it's a game."

"I'll find out what he needs, his sizes, and have my friends help me scout the resale shops for a tux." Mary finds a new tuxedo in Bart's size with a small rip in the lining—marked eighty percent off—she buys it and has the rip repaired. Anna buys him a red bowtie, new black socks, and a fancy silk shirt. He shines his black shoes and is ready for a dress rehearsal.

Friday night, they move the table against the sunroom wall, put on the new clothes, and get ready for a show. Anna will only agree to two dances in the new outfits. "We might rip something and spoil our plans for the date. Two dances and we'll change into our old clothes to practice."

Jackie's boyfriend asks her to the dance, but she says she has nothing to wear.

"Girl," Anna exclaims, "We'll check the resale shops and

find something. You can't miss a valentine dance."

The next Saturday the two girls visit every resale shop in Fayetteville and Springdale. Jackie decides on a lavender dress trimmed in purple. She buys a deep purple bowtie for her date.

"Anna, I'm not an expert dancer. What if I embarrass Jason?"

"You could sit at home and be an old maid saying, 'What if.' You have to laugh and live. He'll love you more for the laughter than if you were a perfect dancer."

Before the dance, Carol circles them, touching Anna's soft dress and whispering wishes that she could go. Bart promises to teach her some dance steps.

The first dance is a waltz. Bart approaches the bandleader, and the next song is a fast one. He and Anna are all over the floor—Anna in the air much of the time. The next five songs are for different dances. A few couples dance; most sit and watch, waiting for a waltz.

Jackie and Jason dance to the waltz. After several songs, Jackie latches onto Bart's arm like sticky tape. "You have to teach me those dances. I'll do anything to learn." She wraps her arms around him, pulling toward the dance floor.

Anna sits with Jason, orders cola and pays the server with money she has taped behind the cummerbund of her dress. Jason shrugs and says, "I don't know what got into Jackie. Is she angry with you?"

"Not that I know of." Anna sips her drink and fans her face with a menu.

"If she's not, you should be furious with her. She's throwing herself at Bart. I'm thinking of taking a taxi home and leaving her here, but we came with you and Bart, so she'd probably applaud that."

Grinning, Anna pats his hand. "You're a good dancer. What dance is your favorite?"

"I used to dance to Rock and Roll with my sister."

"Any particular song?"

"My sister collected over two hundred records. *'Little Bitty Pretty One'* was her favorite."

"If I get the band to play it, will you dance with me?"

"Sure, I can move with that song."

Anna circles the dance floor, whispers to the band director, and returns to Jason at the table. He stands, rips off the purple bowtie, tosses it on the table, and holds out his hand as the band begins the song. Their feet move like automatic machines.

Both old and young disappear from the dance floor as Jason twirls Anna. The band shifts to a waltz without stopping. Jason and Anna stay on the floor—cheek to cheek. The song is almost over when Bart taps Jason on the shoulder and takes Anna's hand. The band switches to "Maybelline." With a grin, Bart spins and yo-yo's her back to his arms. The crowd cheers. Anna does not have time to look at Jason and Jackie.

When a waltz begins, Anna relaxes in Bart's arms. "You're beautiful," he whispers in her ear, "The crowd loves you, and so do I."

She speaks softly, "And I love you."

"I believe you mean that."

"I do. My heart bubbles over with love."

"I was afraid you would be upset because of Jackie."

"I saw what she was doing. I don't understand why, but it was all her doing."

"Look at her now—she's snuggled up to Jason."

"Maybe she decided he's a good dancer."

The two couples dance to almost every song until Bart says, "I'm beat. I got up this morning at four to read an assignment. Are the rest of you about ready to leave?"

Anna and Jason agree, but Jackie frowns. "It's only eleven. The dance is not over until one."

"What time did you get up this morning?" Anna asks.

"Nine; I don't have class on Friday."

Anna takes a deep breath. "Jason what time did you get up?"

"Four-thirty to work on homework, and I'm tired."

"Jackie, you're overruled. Save the dress, you can wear it again. You and Jason look good on the dance floor."

Bart stops the car at a gas station, and the two young men go inside.

Jackie brushes at her skirt. "What are the two of you doing next Friday night?"

"Bart has a class on Saturday morning. We study together, and rarely go out."

"You can't stay home all the time, like old fogies. I'll find someplace where we can go and dance."

"No, Jackie. Bart's taking eighteen class hours—hard classes. Everything else comes second to his studies. Dancing will have to wait."

"I wouldn't stand for that if I were you."

"What do you mean?"

"I wouldn't sit around on weekends and watch him study."

"I admire him for working hard, so he can graduate early, and we can get married."

"Married. I thought that was a friendship ring."

"No; it's for our engagement."

"Well, you better hang on tight, he's awfully cute. All's fair in love and war."

Anna stares at her.

"I'm kidding."

Friday afternoon, Jackie follows Mary into the kitchen. "Hey friend, I finagled myself another dinner invitation."

"I see, but as I told you, Bart and I study on Friday nights. I'll take you home after dessert."

"No, Jason gets off work at ten; he said he'll come pick me up."

"Bart has an early class. He goes to bed at nine."

"You are old fogies."

"We do what seems best to us. I'll take you home after dessert. Jason can come to your apartment."

"Well, sorry. If I'm intruding, you can take me home now."

"Mary invited you for dinner, so you're not intruding, but Bart's working hard for his degree. I plan to help him in every way I can."

Professor Dugan and Bart always sit at the table ends. Mary sits on Professor Dugans right; Carol's chair is beside her on Bart's left. Anna sits on Bart's right. Tonight, as soon as Bart takes his seat, Jackie sits in Carol's chair.

Carol frowns and looks up at her mother. Mary bends and whispers in her ear; Carol goes to sit beside her daddy.

Except for an occasional nod and answering questions, everyone except Jackie eats in silence. Jackie starts to chatter after the prayer. "Bart, you are smart. I know you could make good grades without spending most of your weekend studying. You need to have fun before you become a grumpy old man."

He glances at her and back to his plate. "I want to learn as much as I can about the profession I plan to enter. Anna and I study together. I enjoy learning, especially when she's there beside me." He moves his chair as close to Anna as possible without going around the table leg.

"But you need variety, exercise. You should dance. Why don't you drive me home tonight and give me a dance lesson? Anna won't mind, and I want to learn how to jitterbug. You look smooth on the dance floor. How about it? I'll pay you for a thirty-minute lesson."

Looking at her, he shakes his head. "Can't do it. I have a paper to write and a stack of books to research. Practice with Jason or go to the Fine Arts Department. They can probably suggest someone to give lessons. I have a goal, and I'm determined nothing is going to deter me."

"Jason's not the dancer you are." She lowers her chin, smiles and looks up at him. "And he's not nearly as handsome."

Anna jumps up. "Jackie, help me serve the dessert."

"I haven't finished my vegetables. Why the rush? Carol still has food on her plate."

"Carol always has vegetables on her plate. Eat up. Bart, will you help me?"

He practically leaps from his chair. "Be glad to help."

Anna reaches for his hand and bumps her shoulder against his arm. "Carol and I made strawberry pie and she whipped real dairy cream for the top."

"We might get rich if I gave up engineering and built you a restaurant. You cook better than any place in town."

"I enjoy cooking for people I love, but I don't want to do it full time."

He pulls her around the corner, out of sight to those in the dining room. "How about being my wife?"

She giggles. "Sounds like a good job." She moves close and whispers, "As soon as we have dessert, why don't you excuse yourself and go to your books. I'll drive the flirt home."

He chuckles. "Do I detect a bit of jealousy?"

"About a ton. You don't want to stick around and watch me strangle her do you?"

"She's taller than you."

She gives him a teasing slap. "Taller, but not faster."

"Oh, I see some fire."

"More than you know." She shakes her head. "I don't understand the way she's acting. We were best friends."

Carol comes into the kitchen. "Can I help? I ate most of my food."

"Sure. Will you get napkins and a big spoon for serving the whipped cream?"

Bart slides a slice of pie onto a paper plate and gives Anna a quick kiss. "Please, make excuses to Charles and Mary, and I'll see you in my apartment when you return." After another soft kiss, he is out the door.

Carrying five slices of cream-topped pie on a tray, Anna goes into the dining room. "Bart said, please excuse him, but he has to get going on his report. He works hard at some difficult classes and makes good grades. I'm proud of him."

Jackie frowns and takes a bite of pie. "This is good. Carol, I've never tasted such wonderful whipped cream."

Carol smiles. "Anna let me lick the beaters after she unplugged the mixer."

When the dishes are in the dishwasher, Anna and Jackie put on coats and walk to Bart's garage. "Girl, I'm glad you can drive without feeling as if someone's going to shoot you."

"The detectives tell me that I have no reason to fear, but I'm still afraid. Knowing what those drug dealers are capable of doing, makes it hard to stop looking over my shoulder."

Jackie looks from side to side before getting in the car. "You've got me doing it. I'm sure glad you don't have to testify in court."

"Yeah, but I hate that those boys were killed. Jim wasn't even old enough to drive when he stepped in front of the Devil's wagon."

"He what?"

"Oh, that's another of Mom's sayings."

"Have you seen his grandpa and little Danny since the funeral?"

She nods. "At church. Danny comes to sit with Carol. They color and draw during preaching. He's quiet; otherwise Mary would tap him on the head."

"I'm sure it's hard for them. The grandpa must feel like he failed."

"Maybe. Jim was a big help. Since Mr. Tucker's surgery, Jim did all the yard work and cut wood for their fireplace. People from church have brought them food and two loads of firewood. Danny brings in the wood each night, and he told me he wants to learn how to cook."

"How old is Danny?"

"Ten; I think. He's in fifth grade, very smart, but a little small for his age."

Anna pulls up in front of Jackie's apartment and waits while she gathers the containers of food Mary sent.

"Tell Mary thanks for the invitation." She stands, her arms

full, "Anna, I miss you. I wish Bart would go back to the Marines." She slams the car door and walks fast toward her steps.

Anna sits looking after her, stunned that Jackie would make such a comment.

Chapter Nineteen

Emotions are swirling in Anna's head, as she drives home and parks in the garage. The building is cold, but the underground tunnel is several degrees warmer. "I wonder if I'll feel this safe next spring when snakes come out of hibernation."

She taps on Bart's door. Greeted with open arms and a soft kiss, she asks, "What can I do to help with your research?"

"Let me print what I have, and you can critique the grammar. Then you can grill me on test questions."

At nine-thirty, Bart walks her to the back door. "I'll see you tomorrow afternoon, but I have to do more research."

"During the fall semester, I'd like to join you in the library on Saturday afternoons, but I may have to find a job. Carol will start kindergarten in August."

"If your parents' house sells, you won't have to get a job."

"A realtor called yesterday to tell me that he has a couple interested if I'll drop the price. I don't intend to lower the price. It's a perfect location, close to town, with a beautiful creek. I wouldn't consider selling if Jaeger's Mama didn't live nearby. I never want to live close to her again."

"I'm surprised she wasn't arrested."

"Jaeger and his dad probably protected her, but she's as evil as they were."

"I don't doubt that. I remember her."

"I need to go to the farm and make sure the place is ready for a new buyer."

"Spring break is next month. Can you wait until then, so I can go with you?"

"Sure, if it doesn't sell in the meantime."

She reaches for the door handle. "I promised Mary that I'd stay with Carol in the morning. Will you join us under the trees for a picnic lunch?"

Pulling her into his arms, he kisses her gently. "I'll do that. See you tomorrow at noon."

Saturday morning is warm for February. A light breeze sings through budding tree limbs. Robins scratch and peck at the ground looking for worms and insects. Cardinals and starlings flutter across the property pecking at pecans left over from fall.

Carol's equestrian skills have greatly improved. Anna watches her run Polka around trash barrels set up in the yard. Motioning her over to the playhouse, Anna pats her horse with one hand and the little girl with the other. "You're getting good at barrel racing. By the time you're old enough to enter competitions, you'll be hard to beat."

"I hope so. I want to learn how to train horses."

"You can plan on doing that for fun, but study hard in school, so you can do something to earn money for your living expenses. You're smart enough to become anything you want, even a doctor or veterinarian." She leans her face against Polka's neck. "My dad trained horses. He loved the work but worked other jobs to have enough money to pay the bills."

"I'll be a veterinarian, and then I'll know how to take care of my animals." She drops Polka's rein so the mare can graze new spring grass. "Anna, can we make chocolate chip cookies for lunch dessert?"

"Mary doesn't want you to eat much chocolate. Why don't

we make oatmeal raisin with cranberries and pecans?"

"All right." She grins. "I might accidentally drop some chocolate chips on a couple."

They put the cookies in the oven as the doorbell rings. "Jackie, how did you get over here?"

"Jason dropped me off. He needs to spend the afternoon in the library. I figured you and Carol would let me have a turn at riding Polka, and I might be lucky enough to get a fresh baked cookie."

"They're in the oven. We plan to picnic in the backyard on paper plates. The birds will clean up the crumbs. I made a loaf of yeast bread for our sandwiches. Do you want to slice it while I peel tomatoes?"

"Sure. Where will I find a serrated bread knife?"

"In a drawer, beside the stove. Carol, wash your hands, and you can put cheese on the bread. Put hot pepper cheese on one sandwich and lay it on the red plate, to keep it separate for Bart."

Anna pours sweet, hot, lemon tea into a large thermos and sets four mugs on a tray, with napkins, and a bag of corn chips. On another tray, she puts quartered apples for Polka and dog treats for Curly. At five minutes before twelve, she adds cookies to the sandwich tray and tops it with a cotton dishtowel. "I think we're ready. Carol, will you take the tray for Polka and Curly? You know where to put their treats. Jackie, I'll take the tea and mugs if you carry the sandwiches."

Jackie nods. "Lead the way; I'll follow."

In the warm spring sunshine, they spread lunch on the picnic table. Anna sits on a bench, leaving enough room for another person on either side. Carol snuggles close on her right.

Walking fast, Bart comes toward them. Immediately, Jackie sits on Anna's left. Carol pokes Anna and nods toward Jackie with a big frown.

Bart is within ten feet of the bench when Carol jumps up. "Bart, I warmed you a spot here beside Anna. I'll sit on the other side so I can toss snacks to Curly."

"Thank you, Carol. You're my kind of friend."

"How is progress on your report?" Jackie asks.

"It's going well. I'll finish in time."

"In time for us to all go dancing tomorrow afternoon?"

"No." Frowning, he shakes his head. "Forget about dancing. I have three years of hard work—spring, summer, fall, and winter—before I can think about fun. I want to make good grades, so I'm at the top of my class and in demand by companies seeking job applicants."

Jackie's eyebrows go up a notch. "You'll be a dull old man by then."

"No way—I'll be ready to marry a beautiful redhead with warm brown eyes and raise a Christian family." He puts his arm around Anna's waist and kisses the top of her head.

Bart gives thanks, and they sit quietly eating and sipping hot tea. Bart takes two cookies, refills his mug, and kisses Anna's cheek. "I've got to get back. See you later."

Carol and Jackie take turns riding Polka. Anna taps her pen on a notepad as Carol gives instructions to Jackie. Anna's mind is not on riding lessons.

Holding the pad, she writes what she remembers about her parents' death, the Game Warden, and everything significant to those cases.

- Green paint on the wrecked white car—a small car with little protection when hit at a right angle by a full-size pickup.
- Did the Game Warden go to investigate near Jaeger's home?
- Arkansas Game Wardens drive green trucks. Has the warden's truck been found—if so, where did they find it, and did the sheriff check for DNA evidence?
- Could Jaeger or his dad have been driving that truck? Jaeger has driven in demolition derbies. He would know how to cause the most damage without hurting himself.
- The green vehicle must have traveled downhill at high speed. Was it airborne after hitting a dip in the road? I've hit that dip a few times, but never at high speed.
- From the top of that hill, Jaeger could have seen Dad and Mom approaching, but they wouldn't have noticed a green truck through the trees, especially since they had the right of way.
- It happened on Mom's grocery shopping day, the day her antique shop was closed, and when Dad took care of his errands. They always left home at eight, so they could finish business in time to eat lunch in town. Jaeger could have determined within minutes of when they would be in that intersection.

Taking out her cell phone, she calls Detective Miller and reads the notes to him. "I can't answer all your questions, but I'll call the sheriff, and I won't rest until I find answers."

Picking up speed and growing colder, the wind drives the girls inside. Carol and Jackie help themselves to more cookies and hot tea. Anna takes a package of beef liver from the meat tray; after rinsing, she leaves it to drain and slices a large onion. While the floured and seasoned liver fries, she adds onions to the pan and covers it with a heavy glass lid.

Jackie comes to look in the pan. "What are you cooking with all those onions?"

"Professor Dugan requested liver and onions with mashed potatoes, gravy, and biscuits."

Jackie wrinkles her nose. "I'm glad Jason is picking me up. I don't eat liver. I can't even stand to look at it."

"I don't like it either. Carol and I will eat vegetables and biscuits."

Jackie takes a cell from her purse and steps into the sunroom. Returning to the kitchen, she puts on her coat and gives Carol a hug. "Jason's on his way to pick me up. I'll see you later."

Stirring gravy with her right hand, Anna waves with her left. "Later."

Carol stands with her arms propped on the cabinet. "This is the first time I've ever been glad for you to cook liver."

"Are you going to try it this time?"

"No way. I'm glad because Jackie doesn't eat it. I heard her telling Jason to come get her, and that she wasn't staying because we have liver for dinner. I don't like her anymore. I think she's trying to steal Bart away from you."

"What do you think I should do?"

Carol giggles. "Punch her in the nose and tell her to go away."

Anna shakes her head. "I can't do that, but I don't think he likes her."

"Okay, but I'm gonna watch her when she comes around." She crawls onto a barstool. "Will you make me something besides liver and vegetables?"

"How about chicken and cheese quesadillas? We have leftover chicken in the fridge."

"Yeah." She grins. "I love those."

Bart comes in the back door. "It smells like suppertime. What's cooking with onions?"

Carol wrinkles her nose and shudders. "Liver."

He looks into every pan. "Liver and onions with gravy, biscuits, and green peas—am I invited?"

Anna pats his stomach. "You can have my share."

"Mine too," Carol adds. "Anna's making chicken and cheese quesadillas for me."

"Bart, Carol thinks that Jackie is trying to steal you away from me."

He grins. "What do you think?"

"I agree with Carol."

He pulls her close. "Don't let it worry your pretty head. She hasn't got a chance."

Mary and Professor Dugan come in from the garage. "Who hasn't got a chance?"

"Jackie," Carol says. "She's trying to steal Bart."

"Was she here again today?" Mary asks. "She invited herself to come home with me on Friday."

Anna nods and waves her hand toward the food. "Supper's getting cold. Everyone grab a bowl and head for the table. Mary, I invited Bart to eat with us. He likes liver, and there's plenty. I didn't think anyone, except Curly, would eat the leftovers, and he won't eat onions."

After the dishes are in the dishwasher, Anna walks with Bart to his apartment. She sits with her legs over the arm of a deep blue, overstuffed chair and reads about ancient history. The chair was in her room when she lived with her parents. Rubbing her hand over the bright fabric, she can almost feel her mom's arms slide around her shoulder. Quickly, she dabs at a tear and looks up to see Bart staring at her.

"You are beautiful." He jumps up, flips a switch on her old record player and holds out his arms. The words and music of "Unchained Melody" resonate softly, as their bodies meet and drift around the room.

The music ends, but they stand, still swaying. Anna whispers, "I love that song."

"I remembered; that's why I put it on the machine." He bends to set the needle on the record. "Listen to the words—that's how I feel about you." He sings along with the music.

Smiling, she looks up and receives a soft kiss.

The music stops, Anna lays her head against his chest. "I don't know what to think about Jackie. She's been a good friend, and except for you, I'd share anything with her."

Bart draws in a quick breath. "She doesn't care for me. She wants you to get mad so we'll break up, and the two of you will be best friends as you were last semester, going places in your car and doing things together."

"Do you think she's that selfish?"

"Would it be less selfish to try and take your fiancé?"

"When we met, we were both in need of a friend. I never thought of her as selfish."

"You have a car, gas money, and you invite her to dinner often."

Leaning back to look up at his face she says, "I'm glad I can talk to you. I could never talk to Jaeger. He was always telling me I was stupid, or that I talked like a crazy person. The counselor said Jaeger wanted me to feel inferior because he knew that I was more intelligent than him."

"That's reasonable. He was always a bully, kicking his dog, beating the horses, and tripping smaller kids on the bus. To make something cower gave him a sense of power."

"Each time he hurt me or destroyed something I treasured, I hated him a little more, but I felt sinful because I know God doesn't want us to hate. I wanted to leave, but the drugs took away my willpower, and he said he'd kill me if I tried."

"What happened to your friends from school. Did any of them visit you?"

"Never. I'm sure Jaeger told them not to come around."

He holds her a little tighter and speaks softly. "Your friends are welcome in our home anytime, but we might have to put up a sign similar to those at the Farmers Market; something like *no squeezing the husband*."

She laughs and resets the needle on the record. "Can we have one more dance before you return to your books? I want to hold you tight."

Chapter Twenty

Monday, after her second class, Anna looks across campus to where Bart usually parks—Jackie is in his arms. She grabs a stair rail and stops. A big man, with an armload of books, bumps into her.

"Sorry, girl, I couldn't stop fast enough."

Anna barely hears him and continues down the steps. Looking again before stopping at the bottom, she sees Bart open his truck door for Jackie. Jason stops beside her. "I told you she was after him."

"I couldn't believe it."

"Hey, are you all right? You look washed-out."

"I need a cola."

"There's a machine around the corner. Sit on the step. I'll get you one."

Bart's truck leaves with Jackie. "How could he? How could she?"

Jason brings the cola and sits beside her. "Do you have a class next hour? If you do, it's almost time for the bell."

"Biology lab." She holds the cola can to her face.

"Come on, I'll carry your books. Grab my arm if you feel as if you're going to faint. I've never seen you look this pale. Those two aren't worth your worry. Don't miss class because of two cheats." Blindly, she follows him into the lab, where he drops her books on a table. "I'll see you after class."

Anna does her best to observe her lab partner's work and copy notes before the bell rings. Jason is waiting and takes her books. "Was that your last class?"

Numbly, she nods.

"Did you drive your car today?"

Again, she nods.

"You don't need to drive. You still look pale. I'll drive your car and take you home. My sister will bring me back to get my car."

"I have an appointment with a counselor in fifteen minutes."

"On campus?"

"No, twelve blocks over."

I'll drive you. I don't have another class today."

Mary is in the front office when Anna comes in the door. "Jackie didn't show up for work. Have you seen her?"

"I didn't talk to her, but I saw her across campus. She was getting into Bart's truck." Anna turns, looking around the office. "Where's Carol?"

"In the break room, working a puzzle." Mary frowns. "Jackie's not answering my ring." She grips her phone as if she wants to throw it. "Will one of you call Bart? Maybe he knows what happened to her."

Jason reaches for the phone. "He's supposed to be in class."

Anna goes to the counselor's office, leaving Jason in the waiting room.

The counselor smiles. "Hello, Anna. Did Jackie come with you? Mary's worried. She has a lot of work for her."

"The last time I saw her, she was leaving with my fiancé, in his truck."

"Does that upset you?"

"Before they left, she was in his arms. That upset me. I knew she was flirting, flirting to the point of throwing herself at him."

Anna takes a deep breath. "I was trusting, until today."

"What do you intend to do about that?"

"Return his ring. I don't want a cheat—for a husband or a friend."

"That will be awkward since he lives in the same house."

"He lives in a basement apartment. I'll stay away from him."

"I noticed Jason came with you today. He was Jackie's boyfriend, wasn't he?"

"Last week, but he knew she was flirting with Bart. That relationship is over, too."

"Do you think the two of you might become a couple?"

"No. I don't want to date anyone, and I don't want to talk anymore. I think I'm going to be sick. Will you reschedule an appointment for another day?"

"Let's go to the break room, have a soda and talk for a short while. I can tell you're upset. You don't need to stay alone until you feel better."

"I need that soda, and I need a nap—then I'll be fine."

"I want to check your blood pressure and blood sugar."

"I need that soda first. I feel shaky."

"Let me see your hand." She swabs it with alcohol.

"Oh." Anna jerks her hand away. "I didn't know you were going to stick my finger."

"Hold it out. I need to get some blood on this test strip before you drink soda." After touching the strip to the drop of blood, she wipes Anna's finger with an alcohol swab. "Anna have you ever been tested for hypoglycemia?"

"No. Why should I be tested for that?"

"Do you crave soft drinks or sweet foods, and feel faint, especially when you get frightened or upset?"

She nods. "Yes, I do. My family doctor said that was because I have low blood sugar."

"How long has it been since you ate something besides sweets?"

"Last night at supper. This morning I ate a muffin, and I drank a cola before my last class."

"You need to call your doctor and set up an appointment for a glucose tolerance test for hypoglycemia."

"What will happen if I have that?"

"You'll need a high protein diet and to limit sodas and sweet foods. I have a boiled egg and some cheese in the fridge. You can sit here and eat that while you drink your cola. Then go home and rest. The world looks better after a nap, and you'll feel a lot better on a high protein diet. Hypoglycemia is low blood sugar. A proper diet is very important."

"I fainted several times as a kid. My family doctor said I had low blood sugar and told me to drink orange juice every morning and keep candy in my pocket when away from home. I never thought it was serious, but I don't like this trembling feeling. I'll try to make an appointment next week."

Mary comes into the break room. "Jackie's on the phone, calling from her doctor's clinic. She twisted her ankle while walking across campus. Bart was in his truck studying and happened to look up and see her fall. He took her to the clinic before going to his next class. She wants to know if you'll drive her to her apartment."

Anna grins at the counselor. "Do you think God's testing me?"

"That could be, but I don't think you'll fail."

After taking Jason to his truck, Anna stops to buy two

cheeseburgers, a large salad, and a half-gallon of milk before picking up Jackie and driving to her apartment.

"Anna, you're lucky to have Bart. I've been flirting with him, hoping you two would break up, and we could resume our friendship, like last semester. It was wrong for me to do that. Will you forgive me? Bart told me he's sick of my flirting and doesn't want anything to do with me. He said he considered pretending that he didn't see me fall."

"Although it hurts to know you'd do such a thing, I forgive you." She parks as close to Jackie's door as possible. "Do you think you can get inside with those crutches?"

"I can manage if you'll hold the door open. Your lunch smells good. I wish I'd known you were going to stop, I would have asked you to get something for me?"

"I bought two cheeseburgers and a large salad for us to share."

"You're still my best friend. Let's hurry inside; an apple is all I've eaten since last night."

Jackie does not have a broken bone in her foot. Anna explains the circumstances to Jason, and he agrees to pick Jackie up every morning before class. Anna promises to take her home and prepare lunches until she can walk without crutches.

Mary calls before Anna leaves Jackie's apartment. "Carol wants to go eat pizza. Do you want us to pick you up, or bring you a pizza home?"

"If you have a leftover slice, save it for me. I'm going home and take a nap. If I'm still asleep, don't wake me. I feel as if I could sleep for a week. Thank goodness, I don't have unfinished homework."

"All right; see you later."

In her room, Anna slips out of her shoes, plops across her bed, pulls a quilt up to her chin and is soon asleep. Her purse and cell phone are on the nightstand. She pulls the quilt over her head when the phone rings. It stops and starts three times before she answers. "Hello."

"Anna, this is Detective Miller. I have some news. We have the Game Warden's truck. It was nowhere near where we found him. Two boys in a canoe found it in Cadron Creek. Someone rolled it off a high bluff. Only the radio antenna was above water."

She shakes her head and sits up. "Did you find any evidence of who drove it there?"

"Divers found a woman's shoe inside. We figure she drove to the top of the hill and when the truck began rolling she jumped out losing one shoe. We're hoping to find DNA evidence in the shoe. Whoever drove the truck could be the one that shot the warden, or at least assisted in the murder."

"Did you see the shoe?"

"Yes, it was a navy blue slip-on, an SAS brand."

"Did it resemble a penny loafer?"

"Yes; why do you ask?"

"Jaeger's mama wore a pair of navy, SAS that looked like penny loafers. I bet it's hers. She's the most evil woman I've ever met."

"We'll check it out. I'm hoping for DNA evidence." The detective clears his throat. "Anna, there was white paint on a front fender and the bumper."

"I figured that. Thanks for calling, and will you let me know as soon as you find out about the DNA?"

"I'll do it. If they find evidence in the shoe, they may let the truck rest where it is. Getting it out will be a real problem. It is in a swift water canyon between two rock cliffs. A wrecker can't get near it. I'll keep you informed."

"Is there any way you can check the inside top for some of Jaeger's hair? I figure he's the one who rammed that truck into the side of Mom and Dad's car. He used to drive in demolition derbies."

"We'll check, but don't count on it. Swift water flows through the cab."

Anna is downstairs drinking a cola when the Dugans come home. Carol runs to give her a hug. "Mama won't let me go barefoot on the cold tile floor. I'll go get you some slipper socks so that you won't get sick."

Anna looks at her feet as Carol runs up the stairs. "I didn't realize I was barefoot. I was asleep when Detective Miller called to tell me they found the game warden's truck in Cadron Creek. A woman's navy blue, SAS shoe was inside. They're checking it for DNA. Jaeger's mama owned some shoes like that."

Mary puts an arm around her shoulder. "Was there any other evidence?"

"White paint on a front fender. I bet Jaeger's mama drove that truck into the creek."

"Anna, you need to eat some of this pizza. It has extra meat and cheese."

Someone knocks on the back door. "That's Bart. His class ended twenty minutes ago."

Professor Dugan opens the door. "How did your class go?"

"We took a test covering some difficult chapters. I would have skipped tonight if not for that." He looks at Anna. "Jason told me that you saw me with Jackie and thought we were hugging." He holds up his right hand. "I swear that was not the case. She couldn't walk—I practically carried her to my truck."

She smiles and pats the stool beside her. "I know that now, but I almost passed out when I saw you holding her. Come share this pizza with me."

He stoops to put his arms around her. "Anna, I could hardly concentrate on my test for worrying about you. Jason told me you got sick."

She laughs. "I'm fine now that I know you and Jackie didn't run off together."

He strokes her hair and bends to kiss her forehead. "I could never leave you."

Carol is tugging on Anna's foot, trying to put a sock on it.

Mary pulls Carol to her feet. "Come with me. It's past your bedtime."

As Mary leads her toward the stairs, Carol calls, "Bart, will you put Anna's socks on her, so she doesn't get sick?"

"I'll do that." He throws the little girl a kiss and leans forward to tug thick red socks onto Anna's feet.

The Dugans disappear up the stairs. Anna and Bart return their attention to the pizza.

Anna takes a sip of her drink and stares at Bart's face. "Jackie apologized for flirting with you and told me she was trying to break us up."

"I knew it. So did Jason. I don't think he'll date her again."

"He promised to take her to class until her foot gets well."

Bart raises his eyebrows. "He'll do that because he's a Christian, but he's looking for a new girlfriend."

"I can't blame him. Jackie didn't treat him with respect."

They go into the sunroom with cups of hot chocolate. Anna

tells him about Detective Miller's call. He sympathizes and talks for several minutes about the murder, before telling her that he got an 'A' on his report. "Anna, the week of spring break, let's go clean your parents' house and spend some time with old friends. Aunt Alice will be happy for you to sleep at her home. I'll take a sleeping bag and hang out at your place. I don't want gossip to get started, and I don't want to leave you there alone."

"If Mary has to work that week, I'll need to stay with Carol."

"We can go Friday night and stay Saturday and Sunday."

"That will work. "What do you think about us keeping Mom and Dad's house if Jaeger's mother is found guilty of helping murder that game warden?"

"It's your inheritance. Whatever you want is fine with me."

She leans her head against his shoulder. "I love that place. We enjoyed such happy times there as kids."

"Yes, we did, and it will be a great place for our kids and grandkids."

"As soon as I find out about the DNA evidence in that shoe, I can tell the realtor whether or not to renew the contract to sell."

"Will you have to pay a fee if you tell her to cancel it now?"

"I don't know; she's an old friend of Mom and Dad. I don't think she'll charge unless her boss insists."

"I know it has good memories, but will it have too many bad memories of you and Jaeger?"

"The counselor where Mary works is helping me with those problems. I'm confident I'll eventually overcome his evil deeds—especially since I have you to help."

Bart yawns and rubs his eyes. "Sorry, I got up at four to study for my test, and it's been a stressful day."

Anna slips from her chair, wraps her arms around Bart, and leans her cheek against the top of his head. "I hope I never have another scare like today. I don't intend to share you with anyone."

Bart stands and pulls her close. "You must have felt the way I did when I heard that you married Jaeger. I'll never, intentionally, give you a reason to feel that way again."

The overhead kitchen light clicks on. In her pajamas, Carol stops in the doorway. "Anna will you get me a drink of water?"

"Sure, I will."

Anna turns to Bart, "You need to get in bed so you can go to class tomorrow."

He gives Anna a quick kiss on the cheek and opens the door to leave. "See you later."

Watching Carol drink, Anna remembers her mama getting up on hot summer nights to pour ice water.

Late in the following week, Detective Miller calls to tell Anna that Jaeger's mother is in jail. "DNA evidence proved that it was her shoe in the truck, and the white paint matched that of your parent's car. They didn't find any of Jaeger's DNA in the truck, but water in that location is swift."

Anna closes her eyes and takes a deep breath. "Will I have to testify against her?"

"I don't think so. DNA makes it firm."

Carol is taking a nap, and everyone else is gone. Anna walks through the house wringing her hands. She stops at the kitchen phone and calls Mary. "Do you have a minute to talk?"

"Is something wrong?" Panic shakes Mary's voice.

"No. It's going right. Jaeger's mother is in jail. They found DNA evidence in her shoe, and that white paint on the truck was from Mom and Dad's car. I just need to talk to someone. The news made me feel strange. I don't know whether to laugh or cry."

"I'm glad you called. That woman is where she can't harm you or anyone else. Do you need me to come home?"

"No, I'm fine. Carol will wake from her nap before you could get here. She wants me to help her cook a Mexican dinner for you and the professor. Carol and her cooking lesson will take my mind off everything else."

Chapter Twenty-one

Anna and Bart in the SUV, the Dugans and Danny in the professor's truck, are on the way home after spending the week of spring break at Anna's farm. Anna jumps when her cell phone rings. "Hello." She clicks on the speaker so Bart can hear. "What's wrong, Mary?"

"Carol and Danny are asleep. I need to speak softly. The preacher called to say that Danny's grandpa suffered a heart attack. When we get home, Charles and I will take Danny up to the hospital in our other car if you and Bart will take care of Carol and unload these vehicles."

"How bad is he?"

"Critical. We'll bring Danny back to stay with us. Do you think Bart will mind sleeping in Carol's room on one of the twin beds so that he can be near Danny? That little guy will need someone if the worst happens. Carol can sleep on the cot in your room."

Bart nods. "I'll do anything I can to help."

"We'll do everything we can. See you at the house."

"Anna, I hate to burden you with unloading, but I think I can comfort Danny more than the Dugans. He's been my buddy all week. I want to go to the hospital with him."

"Carol and I can unload. Go with them."

"If Mr. Tucker dies, would you object to me taking Danny?"

"No, but a judge will. The court won't let a young, single guy take custody of a child."

"I can't let him go to an orphans' home. I know what that's

like. I spent time in one after Mom died."

"The Dugans might take him until we get out of school and get married; then we could adopt him."

"You'd want to do that?"

"Certainly, but he may have relatives that want him."

"He said he didn't. He told me that Grandpa is his only relative."

"Do what you think is right."

"What if we need to get married, at the end of this semester, to keep him from going to a home?"

She feels a crease forming across her forehead and a tightening in her chest. "Bart, I love you, but I'm not ready for marriage. Sometimes, I still panic when you hold me tight. The counselor said it might take months before I can overcome Jaeger's abuse. Too much has happened." She wipes away a sudden tear.

"I'm sorry. I promised not to rush you."

They sit without talking until pulling into the Dugans' backyard. Anna grabs an ice chest of food and takes it inside. Bart goes to talk with Danny.

Carol falls asleep, and Anna reads halfway through a mystery novel before the Dugans, Bart, and Danny return. Mary leans close and whispers, "Mr. Tucker talked to Danny before his heart stopped. We promised that we'll take care of Danny."

Bart stays home with Danny on Sunday morning. Sunday afternoon, Bart and the Dugans take Danny to make funeral arrangements. He is familiar with the process. His facial expression seems set in stone as he says, "I helped with the plans for Grandma and Jim. I know what Grandpa wants and years ago, Grandma bought an insurance policy to pay for everything except flowers and the preacher."

Tuesday, after the funeral, Danny is quiet and pale. Anna puts her hand on his forehead. He does not have a fever. "Danny, if you want, you can rest on the cot in my room." He nods and climbs the stairs. Going up to check on him, she finds him holding his stomach.

"My belly hurts."

She grabs a plastic trashcan. "If you need to throw-up, use this can. I'll get a cloth to wash your face."

Mary puts a sleeping bag in her bedroom for Carol so that Danny can sleep on the cot. He is sick throughout the night. Anna bathes his face, keeps the can rinsed, and rubs his back when he moans in sleep. He sits on his cot in the early morning.

Anna forces her eyes open. "Do you feel better or do you need another cold cloth."

"I'm hungry."

"That's a good sign. Let's go downstairs. I'll make breakfast for you. I think a piece of dry toast and some tea is the best thing for you to try. If your stomach doesn't reject toast, you can have scrambled eggs."

Mary and Anna's schedules mesh so that one is always home to care for Carol. It works for Danny as well. Mary calls his teacher to inform her of his situation. Immediately, he is part of the family.

Danny moves into one of the bedrooms Bart constructed in the basement. He never complains about not having a TV or anything else. Every Thursday he, Carol and Mary visit the local library. He brings home an armload of books each week. Words he cannot pronounce he copies onto a notepad, looks them up in a dictionary, and asks Anna about them the next afternoon when she helps with his school homework.

Every afternoon Curly waits on the patio until Danny comes home from school. At night, Curly sleeps under Danny's bed. They find no more snakes on the property, although the dog continues to search.

Anna loves Danny as much as Bart does, but sometimes she longs for the evenings when she went to Bart's apartment to talk and dance to the music of her Mom and Dad's old vinyl records. Most Friday nights, Mary and Professor Dugan go out with friends.

One afternoon Anna asks, "Mary, do you mind if I rent a movie for Carol and Danny to watch on Saturday night while you and Professor Dugan read? Bart and I want to dance and listen to music in his apartment."

"I should have thought of that before. You and Bart need some alone time. I'll let the kids pick out a couple of movies when we leave the library."

In April, when Bart and Anna do not have to study, they drive to the farm on weekends to fish and ride horses. Danny and Carol go along, and sometimes Mary and Professor Dugan. Mr. Prince feeds and checks on the horses every day. They have no vandalism at the farm since Jaeger's family left.

The paper money found buried beside the old stable is purchased by a collector, along with the other collectibles. The Dugans lawyer handles all details of the sale. With her share of the treasure, Carol insists on buying vacant land joining the Dugan property. She also buys a gentle mare with an apple shaped spot on its hip. She names the horse Apple.

Anna tells Bart about the gold and money she has in savings. "I want to talk to the real estate agent and make an offer on the twenty acres joining the five that Carol bought. It has a creek on one side, and abundant trees including large cedar, pine, oak, and walnut. High above the creek, it has a nice flat area for building. I've ridden over it a couple of times."

"Let's ask the owner if we can ride horses over there and look."

Saturday morning, riding Polka and Apple, they go exploring. He loves the property and begins to plan the layout of a house on the flat above the creek.

"Bart." Anna reaches for his hand. "We can't build a house until you graduate. I want to buy this land before someone else gets it, but we can build in a couple of years."

They dismount and stand looking across the valley. "Anna, this place is ideal. I couldn't have dreamed anything better unless it's you sitting beside me on our front porch, but I don't want to wait. Marry me, Anna. We can cancel our summer classes and build a small house during summer break. A few years from now, we can use it as a guesthouse or maybe an office. Life is too short to postpone our life together."

They embrace and kiss. Anna feels no panic when he hugs her tight. She wants to hold him and never let go.

She clears her throat before speaking. "He may not accept our offer, and if we buy this, will we have enough left to build a house, and what about Danny?"

"Oh, hon, we don't need every little detail worked out. Land in this area is expensive, but we'll have enough to build a house and last until we graduate."

"I'm a planner. Surprises make me nervous." She takes a deep breath and hugs him. "I love you; still, we've got to have a house before we get married."

He has a pained look on his face.

"It doesn't have to be fancy. A small one or two-bedroom with a bath will do. Danny will want to stay at the Dugans."

"Maybe, at first, but not for long. That boy loves the outdoors." He looks around. "The real estate company built a paved road near the building site. I can build a house, but getting water and electricity may be a problem."

"They ran electric lines underground along the paved roads, although water and sewer may be a holdup. We'll have to find out about that before we make an offer on the property. Maybe, with twenty acres, the city will let us have a well and septic tank. We'll ask the realtor and double check with the city."

Bart and Anna close on the purchase of the land, withdraw their applications for summer classes, get electricity turned on at a power pole, install a septic tank, have a well drilled and install a water pump. Within a week after Bart's final test of the semester, he and friends from his engineering classes have the foundation dug, water and electric lines run, and cement ordered for the slab.

Anna buys a picnic table and sets up an outside kitchen where she prepares three meals every day for Bart and his work crew. They arrive before six, eat, and begin.

Saturday, the cement truck rumbles up the road before they finish breakfast. Men gobble the last morsels from their plates and stand ready with cement hoes, leveling boards, shovels, and trowels. Carol waits beside the faucet, ready to provide water to clean hands and tools. Danny runs, delivering drinks and supplies to the workers.

Sunday, the foundation is dry enough to walk on. After church, Bart and his friends lay out the framework. Danny works as hard as anyone, running for nails and tools. Carol spends Sunday with her mom.

Professor Dugan drives over to check on progress. "My goodness, I'm amazed that you have the frame in place. By this time next week, it will be ready for furniture."

The men are having a great time joking and laughing. Danny fits in as well as any college boy. "I want to study engineering and learn how to build things. Someday, I want all of you to help build my house."

They nod and say, "We'll do it, Danny. You just let us know when."

Half of the land is outside city limits, with no firearm restrictions. Every evening, before sunset, Bart and Anna practice shooting. Danny and Carol ask to learn.

Anna frowns and wipes her pistol with a soft cloth. "If Mary and the professor say it's okay, we'll teach you, but you *must* do as we say."

Carol squeals, "We will."

Danny frowns and looks at the pistol Bart holds. "I never want to shoot someone, and I don't want to shoot an animal, but I want to know how to defend myself and my family."

Bart crouches next to him. "That's the reason I have a gun. They're not toys." He shows them the parts of the gun and explains how to hold and aim, but will not let them shoot until the Dugans approve. Both Carol and Danny pay close attention and ask questions.

The Dugans give Danny permission, but they want Carol to wait at least two more years.

On Monday, the men put up trusses and lath. Tuesday, they put on the roof. Wednesday, the outside walls go on and are packed with insulation. Thursday, they hang sheetrock and doors, but the doorknobs still wait in boxes when red sun embraces western hills. Tired but happy, the group quits work and packs up tools. Bart and Danny set cots and sleeping bags inside the unfinished house.

"Anna, can we stay in the new house tonight?" Carol asks.

"Not me. I want to be safe in my bed. There are no locks on the doors. Bear or panther might be roaming these hills. Those ice chests Bart has propped against the doors scarcely keep out the wind. A bear could easily push inside. When I can shut wild animals outside, I'll stay."

Danny grins. Bart winks and turns to walk away.

Anna tosses ice from her glass at them. "Laugh all you like. I want locks on my doors."

"Me too. Let's go home, Anna." Carol walks toward the car. "Danny, I hope a bear doesn't get you."

Anna is so tired that she forgets to take the trash to the Dugan house for sanitation pickup. The next morning it is scattered across the yard, and bear tracks surround the picnic table. "Guys, I'm sorry. Did you hear the bear?"

They grin and nod. Danny says, "I was glad we didn't have food in the house. A big bear and two smaller ones prowled through the trash, grunting, growling and having a bear party."

They install locks on the doors and Bart puts in ready-made cabinets. "I would like to build custom cabinets, but I don't have the proper tools. After I graduate and get a decent job, I want a shop building with good woodworking tools."

"My grandpa, Mom's dad, could build beautiful furniture. I don't know what happened to his woodworking tools. They would be antiques now and much harder to use than modern power equipment."

"We would treasure them. Do you have any uncles that might have inherited them?"

"They died years ago. We'll have to build our own collection of treasures for future generations."

Friday afternoon while Danny and Carol go to the library with Mary, Anna and Bart walk through the little house touching walls and looking out windows. "Bart, I love this place. I know we'll be happy here."

"I'm sure of it. Danny said he wants to help me build porches on the front and back."

"Someday, Danny will be good at building."

"He's pretty good now. He watches, listens, and learns fast. I wasn't sure about teaching him to shoot my gun, but he's a natural and very safety conscious. During pioneer days, kids his age went hunting and helped keep meat on the table. Carol doesn't bother the guns, but I've noticed her watching when we practice shooting, and she's very attentive when we talk about safety."

"Danny seems wiser than most boys his age. He's experienced several tragedies. You are his father figure now. You'll have to be careful and set a good example."

"I do my best." He winks at her.

"Carol watches every move you make. I'm not the only one to walk the line."

She nods. "I've noticed. I bet she could cook simple meals without any help, maybe better than Jackie and a lot of college girls."

With his arm around her waist, they walk to the picnic table. In silence, they watch the sky turn a deeper shade of crimson, and the sun slip lower behind the hills. Anna turns to Bart and notices a troubled look on his face. "What's wrong? I can tell a worried look."

"Have you balanced our checkbook lately? I panic when I think about running out of money. There's still a lot I want to do before we move in."

"I balance it every night before I go to bed. As long as you tell me when you order something and what it costs, I'll know our balance. We're fine now, but I think we need to wait about ordering carpet and vinyl—those are expensive items. We can manage on the concrete floors for a while."

He shudders. "I hate to think of stepping out on cold floors this winter when snow's on the ground."

"There are a couple of builders at our church. If you're not too proud for me to ask, I'll see if they'll give me the leftover carpet and vinyl pieces from their new buildings. We can glue the vinyl and tape carpet together with carpet tape and have a warm patchwork floor until we graduate."

"I'm not too proud. We're college kids. Not many students have land and a nice little house like ours."

She hugs him. "Good, I'll call them tonight."

"It's getting dark. We should make sure there is no trash or food in the house before we leave. We don't need more midnight visitors." He laughs. "I think I was more worried than Danny."

Anna hooks an arm around his waist. "Do you remember me telling you that Mary's cleaning lady moved? She gave me that job, eliminating my helping you tomorrow, but I'll get paid—that means more money for our house."

Bart grins and gives her an OK sign. "Now, Danny's my

only steady helper, and we've got a busy day planned."

"Be careful, watch out for those bears, and don't forget to say your prayers. I've got an uneasy feeling—as if something bad is about to happen."

He tosses a sack of trash into the bed of his truck. "It's too late to get cold feet about the wedding. Our house is almost finished." He wraps an arm around her shoulder and looks down at her face.

She pulls him closer. "It's not that. Just take care of my groom and your best man. And remember to pray. I love you, Bart Grayson."

Title: ***Dark Secrets***

- Author: Nancy Powell
- Publisher: TotalRecall Publications, Inc.
- Format:
  Hard Cover: 9781590955857
  Paperback: 9781590955864
  eBook: 9781590955253
- Number of pages:288
- Pub Date: 2013

Ollie's Angels Series Book One

Dark Secrets is the first book in a series based on the life of a farm girl born in 1908 when the United States was becoming a world leader, and farm families made up over half of the population. Conditions for the Negro had worsened, women rallied for the right to vote, and social change in music, dance, and fashion filtered into rural areas. This book shows prejudice faced by Negroes, Gypsies, Jews, and women of that era.

The book begins with Ollie trying to get home after receiving a head injury in an attack by two boys—the same boys that she thinks raped her friend and murdered a girl in a nearby community. She remains in a coma for five days, recalling vivid events of her first fifteen years.

Ollie is competitive and contends with schoolmates, and her older brother and sister, but is eager to help with younger siblings. With a gift for premonition and healing, her ambition is to be a nurse, but when her papa has to pay a promissory note signed for a friend, he cannot afford to send her away to school. With no money for schooling, she worries about becoming a spinster. Still, she rejects all the young men—until she meets Roy.

Title: ***Angels For All***

- Author: Nancy Powell
- Publisher: TotalRecall Publications, Inc.
- Format:
  Hard Cover: 9781590955888
  Paperback: 9781590955895
  eBook: 9781590955185
- Number of pages:288
- Pub Date: 2013

Ollie's Angels Series Book Two

Angels for All is the second book in the Ollie's Angels Series. It continues the story of a young couple in love. Ollie believes in premonitions sent by guardian angels, but has no warning of the hardships to come with drought and the Great Depression.

Roy and Ollie start married life on a sharecrop farm, striving for a better future and a place of their own. Each chapter is an episode that illustrates difficulties imposed by farm life. Almost every year, Roy goes away to other states working to earn money for the mortgage and other necessities.

Ollie stays on the farm to harvest crops and care for the children. She struggles against wild animals, foraging pigs, sickness, storms, hunger, and neighbors that prowl night and day stealing everything they can, including diapers, garden vegetables, harness, and cottonseed.

Ollie offers thanks for blessings she receives, giving credit to guardian angels for helping, but sometimes berates herself for discounting premonitions of impending danger.

Title: *Listen For The Angels*

- Author: Nancy Powell
- Publisher: TotalRecall Publications, Inc.
- Format:
  Hard Cover: 9781590955918
  Paperback: 9781590955925
  eBook: 9781590955291
- Number of pages:232
- Pub Date: 2014

Ollie's Angels Series Book Three

Listen for the Angels, the third book in the Ollie's Angels Series, begins on the road to California where Ollie and Roy move in search of a prosperous life following struggles during the Great Depression. They work at farm labor and Ollie gets a disease that newspapers call Sleeping Sickness. Others have died from the illness, but doctors do not know the cause. Intuition tells Ollie that mosquitoes cause it—she takes a quinine tonic and recovers.

They move back to Arkansas, buy a small farm and continue the struggle of rural life. Almost every fall, Roy goes away to other states to earn money for the mortgage, to buy seed and fertilizer for the next year's crop, and to pay doctor bills.

In 1946, Roy and Ollie buy the farm of their dreams, but drought destroys the harvest. In 1950, while expecting her seventh child, Ollie, gets strep throat and loses her hearing. She is blessed with twins, but four years pass before she can afford a hearing aid to enable her to hear her babies laugh or cry.

Roy tries to borrow money to start a Grade 'A' dairy farm, but cannot get a loan. Fire destroys the pasture, corn and cotton crops, and a tornado hits the farm.

The Roy and Ollie Glenn family, 1956.

Title: ***Protecting the Innocent***

- Author: Nancy Powell
- Publisher: TotalRecall Publications, Inc.
- Format:
  Hard Cover: 9781590955055
  Paperback: 9781590955062
  eBook: 9781590955079
- Number of pages:232
- Pub Date: 2016

The Keeper Series Book Two

Anna heard the report of Jaeger's death, but she cannot believe it and continues to watch for him; he promised to hunt her down and kill her. Neighbor boys, Hank and Bill find themselves in trouble with the Game and Fish Commission, Child Services, and the Prosecuting Attorney, but the Dugans intercede and take the boys into their home as foster children. Also, they take a little girl whose parents were murdered—her biological father was wealthy, and she is in line to inherit a fortune. When she is found by a rich grandmother, more problems arise.

Title: ***Pursued***

- Author: Nancy Powell
- Publisher: TotalRecall Publications, Inc.
- Format:
  Hard Cover: 9781590955086
  Paperback: 9781590955093
  eBook: 9781590955109
- Number of pages:232
- Pub Date: 2016

The Keeper Series Book Three

Neglected for the first six years of her life, Maddi learned to watch for danger. Now, she has found a loving family, but someone wants her to die—her hair is burned, a landslide dumps dirt and rock on her, and she narrowly misses a rifle bullet. Someone is stalking and making her constantly afraid. At school she misbehaves so the teacher will sit her in a corner away from the windows, and at night she hides under her bed. Anna does her best to protect the children, but she still feels pursued by Jaeger's family and the human trafficking cartel.

www.ingramcontent.com/pod-product-compliance
Lightning Source LLC
Chambersburg PA
CBHW030428310726
48979CB00009B/1669/J
* 9 7 8 1 5 9 0 9 5 5 0 2 4 *